D0860312

WITHDRAWN

TRAVELING
COMPANIONS

Friedrich Gorenstein

TRAVELING COMPANIONS

Translated from the Russian

by Bernard Meares

A HELEN AND KURT WOLFF BOOK

HARCOURT BRACE JOVANOVICH, PUBLISHERS

New York   San Diego   London

Requests for permission to make copies of any
part of the work should be mailed to: Permissions Department,
Harcourt Brace Jovanovich, Publishers, 8th Floor,
Orlando, Florida 32887.

This translation has been made possible in part
through a grant from the Wheatland Foundation, New York.

Library of Congress Cataloging-in-Publication Data
Gorenshtein, Fridrikh, 1932–
[Poputchiki. English]
Traveling companions / Friedrich Gorenstein :
translated from the Russian by Bernard Meares.
p.   cm.
Translation of: Poputchiki.
"A Helen and Kurt Wolff book."
ISBN 0-15-191074-X
I. Title.
PG3481.2.R45P613   1991
891.73'44 — dc20   91-12333

Designed by Trina Stahl
Printed in the United States of America
First United States edition
A B C D E

These thoughts of mine,
These thoughts of mine
They weigh me down,
They stand along the printed page
In heavy-hearted lines.
—SHEVCHENKO, "THOUGHTS"

The nightmares that I had didn't need to be invented; they
were nightmares that oppressed my soul; and what was on my
mind came forth.
—GOGOL, SELECTED CORRESPONDENCE WITH FRIENDS

Rarely does the mourning' rite
Strike at the midnight hour,
In its sepulchral metal voice
Toll for us at our wake.
—TYUTCHEV, "INSOMNIA"

1

"JUNE 22, 1941, was the blackest day of my life. That day, at five o'clock in the morning, when I returned home from a trip, I found a rejection slip in my mailbox, from a Moscow theater, informing me that my play, *A Ruble and Two Bits*, had been rejected. The postman had delivered it the day before."

I heard this odd statement in a sleeping car on train number 27, the Kiev–Zdolbunov passenger-mail train, which leaves the Kiev suburban terminal at 7:35 in the evening and arrives in Zdolbunov, a town in the Rovno district, at daybreak the following morning. It is not really a suburban train at all, nor even a regular local. The journey takes ten hours. The train, a fairly low-grade combined mail and passenger service, leaves from the suburban terminal because it runs on a branch line, and stops at every station, without exception, down to the most insignificant wayside places ignored by the expresses. Nevertheless, the service is actually nonstop as far as the first big junction after Kiev: Fastov, a town that is noisy in the daytime and sleepless by night, made so by frequent electric trains that run on the suburban line between it and Kiev. However, once Fastov is behind you, the local electric service becomes infrequent or nonexistent in the evening, and the night train slows down to streetcar pace, delivering mail and passengers to all the villages and tiny townships in the Kiev, Zhitomir, Vinnitsa, and Rovno districts.

Obviously, making leisurely stops at wayside stations during the night on train number 27 is not to everyone's taste in the hectic age we live in. Many prefer to leave Kiev before nightfall and travel by intercity bus down the Kiev-Zhitomir Highway. The better-heeled take taxis. People from the bigger towns and cities, where the faster trains stop, try to get tickets on the more prestigious expresses that run between Kiev and Odessa or Kiev and L'vov. If they manage to find tickets for the Kiev-Moscow or Kiev-Leningrad expresses, train number 2 or train number 3, they buy them, because on these trains they get to ride in cars imported from East Germany or Czechoslovakia, which have compartments with mirrors on the walls. For a few hours they stop being provincial hicks and associate with fine people from the great capitals of the Soviet republics or other major cities. They can join in discussions of politics and art, drink beer, and buy chocolate from the train conductors; and if they are high livers, they can trot off to the restaurant car and indulge in chicken Kiev washed down with Cuban rum.

Those who are still hanging around Kiev at nightfall are welcomed with open arms aboard the night train—as are those whom evening finds exhausted by the city's steep streets and stiff-necked government offices, and those who do not have two or three hours to kill waiting in line for an express-train ticket, and those who are weighed down by bags and purchases of various kinds that you can't stuff into a mirrored compartment, and those who prefer the night train because it's cheaper, and those who live in the villages and small towns of the Ukraine that the Moscow expresses do not serve. They all take train number 27. There are plenty of tickets, and to secure them you don't need to stand in line for hours fighting the crowd and risking disappointment.

If you go down to Pushkin Street to the alternative, the main city ticket office, you will quickly come to a greater appreciation of the Kiev suburban and the welcoming atmosphere of the night train, steeped as it is in the homey odor of salt pork and garlic.

Night mail trains were not always as hospitable as they are now. The elderly or middle-aged will remember prewar, war, and postwar times when the still-new cars were headed by steam locomotives that often stood around for hours, panting smoke up at water towers or having coal poured into them at railway junctions. They will remember the unending stretches of snow or heat-saturated countryside, the interminable stops that were more wearing than the constant juddering and clanging of a moving train. When forward thrust overcame immobility, the trains moved, for the laws of physics were strictly obeyed, like all other laws of those times. Hearts raced toward cardiac arrest and lungs toward pneumonia, and the welfare of the stomach and the pancreas was ignored. In that stifling air, so full of gas and chemicals, with clouds from evil-smelling coarse tobacco faintly stirred by drafts from the platforms at the ends of the cars, it was only the children who howled and complained, because their complaints were not yet subject to the rigor of the law, their ideology being unsound, infantile, and inarticulate. But there were many hearts and lungs that breathed that air, doled out though it was, like rations. And for some reason, ever more children were brought into the world. So life crept on like a troop train: it relaxed whenever the moving wheels hammered out their messages, and worked itself up into a state of mortal weariness during the long stops. It crept on, jam-packed, the motion noticeable not by things passing, but by people getting off or boarding at the various stations. The changing of the passengers served as a milepost; it marked the distance covered and the length of life lived, showing who was no longer present in different decades, the twenties, the forties, the fifties. But the joys and sufferings of those getting on and off were run-of-the-mill, humdrum, and uninteresting to those who remained aboard. Man is fragmented and faceless when there's no one to talk to. The Listener's task is always to tell the Narrator who he really is and how he differs from other people. Not through words but by that inspiration that is the highest form of creation and cannot be appreciated by everyone. It comes from God, like the biblical wind or spirit.

It is no surprise that in the Union of Totalitarian Republics the Listener is considered a troublemaker, a felon, for he fragments the masses into individuals. It is no surprise that the Listener has become an endangered species, what with everybody talking at once, and culture itself perishing in the cacophony. I don't know if I was a good Listener, if I succeeded in my allotted task, but I did patiently devote to the Narrator the entire journey from Kiev to Zdolbunov, even though I had originally reserved a berth in a sleeping car because I was tired and wanted a good night's sleep.

A few words about the sleeping car, to give you a full picture of the circumstances in which this person recounted his life story to me. After all, an account is affected by one's surroundings, whether they be the bright lights of a university lecture theater or the flickering half dark of a campfire on the fringes of a wooded swamp. The setting can make all the difference. The relation between an event and its telling is like the relation between rye and bread, for example. Both are equally real and palpable. But if an event is not told, it has no value; it cannot be digested, even by the person who experienced it, just as rye cannot be eaten by the farmer until it is baked into bread. Moreover, the telling of an event, be it ever so unpleasant, either reconciles people with what has happened or distances them from it.

But about the sleeping car itself. Before standing in

line to buy a ticket, I always go out to look at the train and learn from a conductor which is the sleeping car on the one I'm taking. Those who have been to Kiev know the station square with the big circular flower bed at its center, around which streetcars squeal and trolleybuses spark, frightening people who have come to Kiev from outlying districts. The old gray station building dominates the square with its glass dome. It stands high above the station hill and can clearly be seen several blocks away in Saksagansky Street, which is named after a renowned Ukrainian actor. A series of old houses down this narrow street are hung with memorial plaques showing that at one time or another they were the home of Lesya Ukrainka, the mystic Ukrainian woman writer. She was obviously in the habit of moving frequently, by choice or by coercion. Streetcars screech down the middle of the narrow street before turning in toward the station. Elderly faces staring at the world from behind the house windows include some who look Jewish, although in the Ukraine you can't always tell who's who by his looks. A citizen of Kiev once told me: "I'm Ukrainian by nationality, but Jewish by face."

Yes, I love Saksagansky Street, at least the middle part of it, near the railway station. At both ends, the street merges into dull modern Kiev: Victory Square, the Circus, and various other undertakings sponsored by Nikita K. and continued by Old Bushy Eyebrows. The problem is not simply one of walls and fabric. There is no point in having garnet-red brick walls around the Kremlin if everything about the place, inside and out, makes you avert your gaze. There is no greater disfigurement than beauty desecrated.

And what about the two churches of the Divine Wisdom in the East Slav lands—down here, in the south, Kiev's gilt-domed St. Sophia, the Cathedral Church of the Divine Wisdom; and at Vologda in the north of Russia, the other Church of the Divine Wisdom, less well known but equally moving, with its silver dome? The golden domes of Kiev's St. Sophia shine brightly through surrounding chestnut trees. Tourists giggle in the old cobbled courtyard, and their bored eyes rest on this place of worship that has been turned into a state museum. Not far away, the equestrian statue of the anti-Semite Bogdan Khmelnitsky, erected by the anti-Semite sculptor Mikeshin, gallops toward Moscow. Khmelnitsky quarreled with the then superpower Poland and handed over the Ukraine to the future superpower Russia. In fact, the place where he swore his allegiance to Moscow was on a Moscow street that now bears his name, in a church that is now a military design bureau, entry into which is prevented by security guards. All you can do is read an inscription on a tablet honoring the event, the garage sale of a state that might have become a Slavic Germany or France. As you read the inscription, you remember the words of Poleshchuk, a Ukrainian satirist of the 1930s: "The enslaved can always rebel, those who have been bought can only be sold." Poleshchuk disappeared soon after making this remark; it was the thirties, after all. The Kiev NKVD building stands guard amid the same ancient chestnut trees, a few minutes' walk from the gold Sophia and the three-hundred-year-old equestrian Russifier. After the union with the fatted lands of the Ukraine, Russia stopped living off its own resources and began its career of outward expansion and dissipation—which it has continued ever since. No good came of trying to alloy the gold of the non-Russian south with the silver of the Russian north.

The silver Sophia at Vologda in northern Russia looks especially charming amid the birch trees in winter when it is sunk in drifts of snow. Even on a rainy gray summer's day the domes on its lofty bell towers are a lovely silver too. The only problem there is the drunks who create mayhem around the stout old timber houses of Vologda, which have carved wooden balconies, eaves, and architraves. These drunken louts in coarse padded jackets blaspheme even by the fences in the shadow of the silver Sophia. The church's thick walls are not much help, although until they are torn down, there is still hope that they can survive the storm, outlast the onslaught. When you come to think of it, it would have been far better to have had drunks around the Savior's Cathedral in Moscow than the Olympic pool that it was pulled down to make way for, a place where the Soviet petty bourgeois self-importantly swim laps. A drunken hooligan is merely a partisan in the Soviet cause: he comes, he shuffles around, and he leaves, unless he is jailed. But the petty bourgeoisie that the Soviet state has created is its regular army.

They are strongly entrenched in the old building of the main Kiev railway terminal, and they are there in force in the city ticket office on Pushkin Street. Their strength is felt not only when they drink beer in the restaurant at the terminal or leaf through the pages of glossy magazines, but also during the tortured wait on line to purchase tickets for the expresses: the Moscow, Leningrad, L'vov, and Odessa trains.

There are at least a dozen ticket windows, and a line of fifty human backs attaches itself to each, like a leech. For an hour or two the people stand crumpled and cramped, until at last a window flap opens and noises begin.

"For the sixteenth of this month, one ticket to Moscow on the number two."

Silence. The ticket agent's fingers dial a number. The mysteries of the telephone. She whispers. The heart beats. What will be the reward for two hours of torment? A sudden explosion. A tinny voice from outer space. "Number two. Gubble-gabble-gubble." That's Central Reservations squawking down the line at the ticket agent.

"No room on the number two to Moscow," a tired voice translates into real Russian.

"Why did Russia annex the Ukraine if there's never any room on the train from Kiev to Moscow?" Even the Soviet species of petty bourgeois can lose its temper if it is unfed, unwashed, and on its feet since early morning. "I'm a Soviet citizen, you know!"

"So?"

"So where are the tickets? This is the first day for reservations for the sixteenth."

"Party booking."

And that's that. It takes more than bare hands to fight armored tanks. The petty bourgeois acknowledges defeat.

"Can I speak to Nelly Pavlovna?"

No one listens. The next customer is already talking with the ticket agent. "Twenty-first on the number three to Leningrad." Outside, Kiev stands, a thousand years of Christian civilization, Saint Vladimir and his cross. But inside, it is Persian misrule.

Stalin's tribe was of Persian blood. The Christian religion never Europeanized the Georgians. The Georgian Orthodox church is dominated, not by the cult of Christ or the Virgin Mary, but by Saint George. The ancient astral cult is still strong, the Persian cult of the warrior slave, the slave assassin.

Far better to be the bondsman of Saint Vladimir than the slave of Stalin the Persian. Far better to use the Kiev suburban terminal, with its pagan, woodland-and-steppe aroma of pork fat and garlic. Far better to take that drab old passenger mail train to Zdolbunov than the Stalinist special, the Moscow express, with its gleaming mirrored compartments. At the Kiev suburban, even the ticket agent will smile at you and wish you good evening. A friendly polyglot, her words emerge in Russian or Ukrainian, sometimes in both at once.

"Which carriage do you want?" she asks.

"Car 11: today car 11 is the sleeping car," I reply.

"That's fine then. Here you are."

"Thank you."

Everything is unhurried. It is like the ancient days of

the Crimean salt trade, when the switches cracked "Saddle up! *Tsop! Tsobay!*" as they say in the Ukraine instead of giddyap. There's time to go out to the platform, find the number of the sleeping car, and return to the ticket office to purchase your ticket and reserve the berth of your choice. You can make yourself comfortable and, before going to sleep, have a snack, spread out on the Kiev evening paper, while the cars are jolted backward and forward along the platform, lurching and screeching like haycarts.

The sleeping car on this train is unlike those on any other, because, for reasons of economy, the lights are never turned on, not anywhere on the journey. Those who want light should find a seat in another car, where the lights will at least be on at half power. You can't read, but you can play cards. And what better activity than cards for the passenger who is crushingly bored by a long journey that he knows like the back of his hand? You can discuss politics, of course, but that kind of talk is as familiar as the journey itself. I prefer to sleep, and if anybody wants to talk to me, I reply politely but sleepily, and then begin to snore.

That was my intention on the present occasion too, after an initial exchange of trivialities with another passenger. And that is how I would have behaved had he not said what he said about June 22, 1941. Those words, which I quoted at the beginning of this chapter, forced me to raise my head and look at the speaker.

He had not spoken immediately, perhaps because he too was intent on eating his supper on a spread-out newspaper before going to sleep. In any case, at first we sat at opposite ends of the nearly empty car. As the new apartment buildings on the bank of the Dnieper slipped by, I ate my supper without lifting my head. I could see them all in my mind's eye, I knew them by heart: the lights on the Pechersk heights and in the valleys of Podol and Kuryonovka, and the twinkling street lamps amid the foliage of parks and squares. The streets running off the Kreshchatik, Kiev's main street—the Nikolayevskaya, Aleksandrovskaya, Fundukleevskaya, Proreznaya, Bibikov Boulevard, and the Great Vasilkovskaya—blinked out of existence like the lights on a chandelier. All that was left of the Kreshchatik was its name, too old to touch—although apparently they tried to take that away too, and had dreamed up some alien, resoundingly Soviet name. But, as with Nevsky Prospect in Leningrad, moderation finally carried the day. (Though in Moscow, the Tverskaya became Gorky Street.)

Old Kiev used to be a city of contradictions, unusually showy but one of the most beautiful cities in Europe, whereas modern Kiev is a monotonous place that has no soul, only a façade. Looking through the window of the train in the twilight, I felt that the spirit of old Kiev now lay at rest amid its sandy hills and at the bottom of its deep ravines. The landscape of the city and its surrounding countryside is extremely broken, with a multitude of hillocks, a geographical particularity that solved many problems for those whose business has been mass execution and mass burial.

When I finally raised my head from the greasy evening newspaper covered with eggshells and sausage rind, the bridge across the Dnieper that keeps the city separate from its suburbs was already behind us. Far off on the horizon, the lights of Darnitsa blinked like sleepy eyes; Darnitsa, along whose sands I had dragged my feet in my youth. There, moving from one building site to the next, I had composed my first poem, in the style of Mayakovsky's "It's Marvelous, All Right":

> *Above my head, the great blue sky*
> *Is marvelous, all right.*
> *On my left, the frosted bridge*
> *Is marvelous, all right.*
> *On my right, the modern factory wall*
> *Is marvelous, all right.*
> *There, the new town of Darnitsa*
> *Is marvelous, all right.*
> *Though old Kiev is backwoods country now,*
> *It's marvelous, all right,*
> *Ukraine and Russia are both one:*
> *It's marvelous, all right.*

When I took this to the newspaper, reverentially, like a believer entering a church, the Ukrainian Cossack editor said: "You shouldn't joke about such a delicate subject." As he spoke I had the impression that he was a ventriloquist and that a voice, rising up from his stomach, shouted the word "Yids!" at me.

But he wasn't a ventriloquist, and the voice, coming from the corridor, was that of Shlopak, a well-known Ukrainian literary critic, his face mottled from drinking pepper vodka, and as red as good garlic borscht. Shlopak was being gently led along by the editor in chief, who was whispering something into his ear, evidently trying to persuade him to go home, take off his shoes and jacket, and drink pickled cucumber juice for his hangover.

"And who's that?" Shlopak's crazed pogrom eyes fixed on me. "Is he one of us?"

"Of course, of course," said the editor in chief, a famous Ukrainian literary figure.

"One of our own Yids, you mean!" Shlopak shouted.

"He's just one of us, one of us," the editor in chief muttered soothingly, as one would calm a wayward child, but giving me a shamefaced glance, as if the child had farted in front of strangers.

Later, I came across an epigram about Shlopak, published in a minor Kiev magazine on his birthday. It included some lines about a conversation between him and a young writer:

> *The critic Shlopak said Sosyura*
> *Had among writers the most bravura.*

For some reason this couplet kept running through my head, along with other nonsense in a similar vein. I sometimes set it to the music of "The Proud Varangian": "Our brave vessel will not flag, never mercy or pity beg. . . ."

Our past, however, is the stuff of dreams, and dreams, nightmarish, pleasant, stupid, or funny, cannot be regimented. In this case, as I stared out at the dying embers of Darnitsa, banked for the night in its sands, it was a dream from early youth that had come to me.

Trukhanov Island now appeared in the warm August twilight, with a whole fleet of boats—yachts and small sailboats—moored in the lee of the land. Rows of sandy hills disappeared into the distance, and drier land began between the riverbank and the area of woodland and steppes, drier but still watered by a multitude of rivers and streams: the Uzh, Irsha, Ros, Olshanka, Zhitomir Teterev, Berdichev Gnilopyat; and then Ukrainian streams, with names like the Sinyukha, Kamenka, Rastovitsa, and Yatran, as in the song that goes:

Where the Yatran swiftly flows,
From beneath a sycamore,
There a black-haired maiden took
Water from the rushing brook.

I love Ukrainian songs, I love the features of old Ukrainian women, and I love the early-melting spring in the southwest, the long hot summer cooled by west winds, and the warm dry fall.

But the Ukrainians themselves I do not love, though that is another matter. Why not? you ask. Please don't make me explain. I think certain thoughts and feelings are murdered by explanation; they become banal, or create misunderstandings. I love the small details and particular facets of an individual more than his personality as a whole. Such details, it seems to me, are from God, but the overall personality, that is the work of the

15

Devil. And the world, taken in its particulars, is a marvel, but viewed as a whole, it is horrifying and sad, like an unquiet spirit wrenched from the fruitful chaos of the Lord into an overripe kind of order that's of no earthly good to anyone.

2

I SHOULD INTRODUCE myself. Zabrodsky. You don't need to know my first name, at least not yet. A first name is too intimate, and, rather than being on intimate terms with someone who is like me, I would prefer to deal with someone who is not like me. If we're different, you can tell me who I am, at least to some extent, by turning things inside out. If you do one thing, I'll do another. But, at the same time, we may be alike in some ways. Resemblances, differences may be clear or unclear. At any rate, comparison between us should not focus on our actions. A man should never be judged by his actions. And if you insist on judging him, bear in mind that your judgment will be superficial. The same action can spring from different feelings and, conversely, the same feeling can give rise to different actions.

Well, all the way to Zdolbunov I listened to my traveling companion, and I was quite happy to have played the part of sympathetic Listener. I don't quite recall how we came to be sitting opposite one another; certainly we did not deliberately pick each other out. In the darkness of the car we had simply groped our way to seats that were less subject to the wind blowing through the windows. I didn't intend to go to sleep before reaching Fastov, and neither, perhaps, did my traveling companion, to judge from the way he moved about in the darkness and groaned, shuffling things in and out of his pockets and doing up and undoing buttons. At a certain point, something fell to the floor with a wooden clatter; and he said his first words to me.

"Sorry. I hope I didn't wake you."

I replied that I hadn't been asleep. It wasn't worth going to sleep before Fastov, since, with the bright station lights and all the noise, you'd get waked up anyway. But after Fastov come Stavishche, Boguiki, Paripsy, Popelnya, and Brovki, all quiet places, plunged in darkness, and you can go on sleeping even when the train stops. And then there are almost five hours to the next major junction, at Kazatin, so you can really get some shut-eye.

"I come from these parts too," he said in answer to my display of local knowledge as he bent down clumsily to pick up the object that had fallen to the floor. It was the kind of walking stick that lame people usually use. The shape of his body, visible through the gloom, seemed crooked, and he was sitting the way cripples sit, his left foot stuck out and twisted unnaturally. So he's lame, I thought. I don't know why I thought the detail merited particular notice, but anyway we started talking, I in fact initiating the conversation, thinking that pointless railway talk as far as Fastov would be a soothing preparation for the sleep I so desperately needed.

But empty small talk with a complete stranger is as exhausting as anything else you do against your will. I have got into this kind of fix on a number of occasions and am always relieved when I can at last fall back into total silence. Even people who have never had such conversations will recognize the interminable pauses, the sighs and vague yeses and noes and well, I sees. Knowing all the while that it's an exercise in futility, both parties keep the phony conversation going because neither has the courage to break it off and honestly turn his back on the other. And the longer it continues, the harder it is to keep it going. Words become difficult to put together into sentences, and finally you think you are forgetting the alphabet. But what can you do? If you're stuck in a conversation of this kind and don't have the courage to break it off, all you can do is try to find subjects you can talk about sincerely, colored with language you would normally keep to yourself or limit to the hearing of intimate friends. This doesn't mean you have to pour out your innermost secrets to the first person you encounter. You can talk, for example, about the countryside flashing past the train window in the twilight, just as long as you speak so that you feel your heart thump and your spirit throb.

I watched a silted-up pond slip by, a pond whose existence could only be inferred from the way the moon glinted on its surface and from the smell of waterweed drifting into the train on the breeze. Leaning on my elbows against the open window, I stared for several minutes, inhaling the damp air and turning my head to hold sight of the pond until it was lost to view behind blurry trees. Then, as if I had forgotten that the person facing me was a casual stranger and not a bosom friend, I uttered the sort of emotional nonsense you tend to lapse into when your thoughts are distracted. But even such talk can set somebody off, somebody who carries his past around with him wherever he goes, like a sack he doesn't know where to empty. It was in this way that my neighbor suddenly started speaking.

I soon discovered he was from the village of Chubintsy, between Belopolye and Skvira and almost a hundred miles from the place we were passing through. I said I knew the area, Belopolye being well known as the site where a Young Communist food-requisition unit from the Cheka had been shot, down to the last man, shot, butchered with axes, and skewered with pitchforks. A film on the subject had been made in Kiev. But as soon as I mentioned the film, I realized that it was called *Tragedy in Tripolye*, and although the incident had taken place in the vicinity of Kiev, it had been in Tripolye, not Belopolye. But the name was known to me for other reasons; first, because I used to pass through it when going to Skvira on business, and second, because the main street in Berdichev, a city I knew well, had been called Belopolye Street before being renamed for the German revolutionary Karl Liebknecht. I was on the point of admitting my error, when my traveling companion said he knew all about the massacre of the Cheka unit in Belopolye, because he had been born in 1920 and was twelve when it happened. He even recalled how bits of mutilated bodies had been fished out of the village pond, an arm here, a head there, for a solemn burial accompanied by a band.

"Belopolye has a beautiful pond," he said. "It's like the one in Chubintsy. There's a multitude of small rivers and brooks around here, and ponds have been dug along them, though they've all silted up long ago, due to poor dam maintenance and to the general plowing of land during collectivization. In Chubintsy the soil was black and always rich, and the village was rich too and surrounded by gardens. It was also rich in cattle, since there was good grazing land all around. They mainly grew wheat and rye, and did some distilling. Home brew from beets came to the village later, just before the famine, but at that time most of the beets were taken to the sugar mill at Skvira."

He was a good talker, and I would have gone on listening without getting bored (though no farther than Fastov, where I intended to fall asleep), but then came his remark, apropos of nothing, about June 22, 1941. He was saying that, despite the mild climate around here, June was always the most worrisome month for the peasants, because frequent heavy rains flattened the grain and caused the beets to rot. Then he said that he personally had unpleasant memories of June, and of June 1941 in particular, that is, of June 22, when a reply from a Moscow theater shattered the hopes of the young peasant playwright he then was.

His name, he said, was Alexander Chubinets. "But half the population of Chubintsy is named Chubinets. Some of us are kin, and some of us simply have the same name. To tell you the whole story would take us all the way to Vladivostok, not just to Zdolbunov. Besides, you know from your school history books about the hardships and the excesses that occurred during collectivization, so I don't have to explain what all our family died of by 1934. It was a big family too: father, mother, brothers, and sisters. But not all the old people had died before 1934; my great-grandmother Tyoklya was still alive. We were sturdy folk, a family of plowmen. I was the only exception, the runt of the litter. When I was five, I fell down a well. I was rescued, but was ill for a long time afterward. You know the kind of medical care you get in the country. Complications from a cold set in. And I've been lame ever since. This was what set me apart from my family. My brothers made fun of me, and the boys in the street nicknamed me 'Ruble and Two Bits.' I'd be hobbling along, and they'd yell after me, 'Ruble and Two Bits, Ruble and Two Bits, you'll never earn a dime!' And my brothers and sisters would all yell along with them. I couldn't complain to my old man, or my mother, or my grandfather or grandmother: only to my great-grandmother. She was the only one who loved me. She couldn't walk much, and spent most of her time lying down, during the winter on the stove and during the summer under our old plum tree. I would hobble up to her in tears and bury myself in her bony arms. And she looked after me in my misery. 'Sasha, little Sasha,' she would murmur, saying my name over and over, but saying it tenderly, and that was enough. She was the only one I loved out of the whole family, and when I discovered that every last one of them had died, I mourned only for her.

"I had already run away from home when the famine began. I couldn't handle their jeers anymore, and also I threw a stone at my elder brother that cut open his head. For that, my father punished me severely, because my brother was by then a capable plowman and was needed. My father gave me a beating that was, as we say, 'three pails worth,' meaning that the first time I fainted, he threw a pail of water over me, the second time another pailful, and then a third. Three pails in all. The bruises took a long time to heal, since tiny splinters from the switches he used remained stuck in my body. I moaned and wept, particularly at night; but this time, not just my great-grandmother but also my mother and the midwife, who was named Christy, took care of me. They treated me with herbs and washed my wounds with grain vodka. But as soon as I was better, I ran away from home, from Chubintsy to Belopolye.

"There was a railway station there, really just a wayside stop, with storage sheds, where I lived with other homeless boys and beggars. While living there, I met a fellow villager who had once been a successful farmer but was now a tramp. He was the one who told me that all my family had died. People were dying in Belopolye too, because the homeless had nobody left to beg from and the young boys no one to steal from. They stole small stuff, trifles. They grabbed something and ran. But you needed good legs, and mine weren't any good. So all I had to live off were the leftovers from what was stolen. Sometimes I'd be given a lump of sugar to nibble or a few grains of wheat to chew. I remember once that somebody poured some sugar into the palm of my hand, and I took all day to eat it. Just touching it with my tongue was bliss. My dream was to kill a bird. A man told me that he had once killed a fat finch in the bushes with a stone. He had plucked its feathers, stuck a spit through it, and roasted it over a fire. I was drooling as he told me the story. But to kill birds you needed good legs too. Anyhow, there were very few birds left, except skylarks, which you couldn't get at because they flew so high. So I realized that I would have to die. I was already vomiting and had diarrhea, although it was a puzzle where my body could find the raw materials for either. The diarrhea was not the kind a well-fed man gets from sour milk. It was black with red spots of blood in it. There was blood in my vomit too. There you are, I thought, a life snuffed out at fourteen. What a pity!

"Incidentally, I had completed three grades in the village school. Although the other kids used to laugh at me and call me 'Ruble and Two Bits,' I liked school. I especially loved fairy tales. I remember that whenever the principal or some big shot came to hear our lessons, the teacher would always call on me. 'Who wrote Tale of the Goldfish?' he would ask, and I would answer, 'Mr. Pushkin.' Of course I didn't have much of an idea then of what poetry was. Even in prosperous times, the average person living in the country had no knowledge of poetry. A plowman's life was made up of totally different pleasures. I felt that maybe there were reasons for my lameness, for my inability to plow, and for the insults I suffered at the hands of others; that there might be a reason I had been born. But reasons or no reasons, I knew I would die, die with my head spinning but fully conscious. I probably would have died too, perhaps a week later, perhaps a month. There were corpses strewn everywhere in those days, and our yeoman farmers, who had kept their pride intact until recently, were not ashamed to lie down and die right in the middle of the street.

"Somehow or other, I gathered enough strength to hop a freight train to Skvira in the hope of finding something to live on, because hope remained alive in me. Often nothing but hope saves you. There, at the station in Skvira, I ran into Grigory Chubinets, who not only came from my village but also had the same last name. He was a former Red Army man with one arm, a disabled veteran of the Civil War. He used to visit us, bringing gifts, because he wanted to marry my mother's younger sister, Aunt Steffie. But Steffie refused him, because he was something of a drunkard as well as a cripple, and she was good-looking and hoped for a better match. Incidentally, like my great-grandmother, Steffie felt sorry for me. In the late 1920s, when the great fuss over collective farms began, she left the village and got work on some Young Communist League engineering project.

"Skipping the details, let me just say that it was thanks to Grigory Chubinets that I survived to see this evening, to find myself traveling with you on the night train to Zdolbunov. He took me in and taught me his business. 'Took me in' is a figure of speech, because I still lived in abandoned freight yards and had to warm myself at small bonfires or in the generating plant for the locomotive sheds. But I really did learn his business. Which was one way of getting bread in those lean years—or I should say meat. Using his wartime honors and hero's scars, he, with the local butcher and the butcher's wife, used to get meat, cook it, and sell it on the black market. Sometimes they took it out to passenger trains, mostly at night, when the controls were not so strict. But Grigory Chubinets was always on good terms with the inspectors. In their Red Army greatcoats and peaked caps—Budyonny caps in winter and forage caps in summer—these inspectors looked just like him. The only difference was that Grigory's sleeve was pinned to his coat. I remember he even got along with the prison guards in charge of the cattle cars that transported prisoners; he'd go up to them in a friendly manner and share his tobacco and talk politics. He once struck up a conversation with a soldier who had a big well-fed dog on a leash. The Red Army man was friendly, but the dog suddenly started barking at me and straining at his leash. I don't know if it was Grigory or me who spooked him. I felt the animal's breath in my face, saw his teeth, like needles in his wide-open maw. Thank goodness the soldier kept him off us. But Grigory didn't care—he laughed. 'He's a good dog. He knows where to get his Sunday roast,' he said. Grigory was a happy-go-lucky type who loved to eat to the point of gluttony. The meat he sold was still red and cooked with garlic. I remember wanting to sing the first time I ate it. I opened my mouth to do so, but suddenly vomited, though by now there was no blood and I was throwing up real food rather than my own guts.

"My work wasn't easy. I had to carry the stuff around in sacks, and sometimes, when Grigory managed to get a wagon and horses, I had to drive. And the work got harder as time passed. Grigory would get raging mad, and more often than not his breath smelled of eau de cologne rather than the usual alcohol. Sometimes I would turn up at the appointed place and Grigory would say there was no work today. If there was no work, then there would be no meat. I'd go hungry again, although not as badly as before, and within a day or two he'd bring me something to eat.

"One day, he said to me: 'There's no work, but I can feed you.' He suggested we go to a small patch of woodland not too far from the station and cook meat on a spit. It was growing dark; it was August and the days were getting shorter. I don't know why, but something made me not want to go with him. He was already very drunk and looked agitated. But, driven by hunger, I relented. Now that I was used to having a full belly and eating meat every day, I could no longer stand hunger, and my thirst for life was once again strong.

"We sat down and made a fire. There were no matches in those days, but we knew how to strike sparks from flints. Grigory took a lump of meat from a bloody piece of cloth and skillfully began to roast it after threading it on a bayonet. All the while he did this, he was gulping down eau de cologne. Suddenly he began talking about the Civil War. 'We had a rule in the war: one half dies and the other half wins. The first half died on the barbed wire and the other half trampled over their bodies and stormed the Perekop isthmus. That's what's happening now: in the fight against famine, half the nation must sacrifice itself for the other half so that not all will die.' That was what he said. And then he pulled the cooked meat from the fire. He chewed and I chewed. He took a swig from his bottle, and I just kept on chewing, thinking to myself, Drink to your heart's content; it'll give me time to eat more than you. He said: 'The meat's fresh, you see, because I don't take sick ones. No matter how much garlic you use with the sick, they still stink of death. The babies are all chicken bones, the old are too tough and oily . . .'

"I gagged on the meat from horror. I coughed, trying to spit it up. He wasn't worried. He knew I was lame and couldn't run very far. And although he had only one arm, he was sturdy. 'That's enough,' he said. 'You've eaten enough human meat. Now lie down on the barbed wire like our comrades at Perekop so that those who follow after can enjoy victory.' When I heard the words 'human meat,' a piece of it jumped out of my throat. Ever since, I haven't been able to eat meat in chunks, chops especially. Sausage is all right, but nothing unprocessed. I've had my ups and downs in life. I was in prison camp for seven years once. But even there, when I found an occasional lump of meat in the soup, though I knew it wasn't human flesh, I still took it out of my soup and traded it for bread. Back in August of 1934, there was good reason to believe that I wouldn't get the chance to taste the joys of prison life or of being a beggar or any of life's other little pleasures, but would instead die on the three-sided blade of a Red Army bayonet. Grigory Chubinets had a wooden arm, into which he fixed his bayonet like a dagger. I'm sure all the meat he sold had been obtained by the use of that bayonet. Only later, it turned out, had the professional butcher begun working with him, in the cellar of his home in Skvira. The butcher did the skinning and the cutting: bones to one side, flesh to another, heads and giblets in a separate pile. Then his wife, the cook, passed the meat through a grinder, along with some garlic. I've seen my share of life's horrors and sorrows, but whenever something reduced me to tears, suddenly the image of that grinder would leap into my mind. And the thought that because my illness had kept me from becoming a true peasant, I might have been better off being born a farm animal. At least I would have been useful as food. Young meat passed through the grinder with garlic . . . The reason we don't eat human flesh is not because it's bad for us or because we're more civilized than the Zulus. The reason is deeper. Don't you agree?"

"Yes, of course," I said hastily. But I thought: The

quicker we get to Fastov, the sooner I'll be able to see what you look like.

I wanted to see this man's face under the bright lights of the station, and also to stretch my legs and drink some water. My original idea of buying beer or lemonade at the station kiosk had lost its appeal. I thought I'd feel sick if I had either.

As we approached the station—Fastov, or Hvastiv in Ukrainian—the lights fell on my traveling companion. I saw that his embroidered Ukrainian shirt covered a hollow chest and that his wrinkled trousers were of cheap denim. Instead of a suit coat, he had on a cotton jacket. If it had had a zipper, it might have passed for sportswear, but, instead, it was fastened with very ordinary, very sad-looking buttons. I also noticed a beret hanging on the hook by his seat. He was pitifully, yet somehow pretentiously dressed. After another minute or so, the train had passed the outer signals, and the brighter station lights flickered across his face. I saw a receding forehead, badly shaved cheeks, and curly fair hair. Then suddenly, in the glare of the Fastov platform, which fully illuminated the picture that until then had hung before me in deceptive half-light, I saw coarse features transformed into fine features, as happens often among degenerates and outcasts, who have lost what is naturally theirs without replacing it with anything copied or acquired from others. Such feral faces occur among wild animals raised in captivity, who are incapable of acquiring the security and appropriateness of a cat or dog in domestic surroundings, but who would be even less at home in the forest. Yet this paradox of their lives endows them with a certain unthinking spirituality. Anyone with a heart feels a desire to nurture such lost creatures, despite the warnings of zoologists and veterinarians that to do so is useless, if not downright dangerous.

Yes, this elderly man seemed like some helpless wild animal cub you could neither abandon in the middle of the highway nor allow in your home. Or so I felt when I had my first good look at him, after hearing his life story up to the point where human flesh saved his life. I realized I would now have to play the role of Listener all the way to Zdolbunov. But for the moment I wanted some water and the respite of a short walk up and down the platform. I was also curious to see how my lost animal would behave in a crowd. He seemed to disappear totally among the people on the platform, assuming the general characteristics of the Fastov passengers, not even his lameness marking him as different, since several other people had canes or crutches. We went to the toilet at the end of the platform and then to the room with a water heater and tap, where I filled my thermos.

He tasted it and said: "It smells of chlorine, no? I think I'll wait until Paripsy for a drink. Right next to the station there is a well that has terrific water."

We were at least an hour from Paripsy, the station after Stavishche and Boguiki. So I drank down two thermosfuls of Fastov water, despite its poor quality. I was extremely thirsty—I always am when I'm seized by pity for some poor needy soul, one for whom, nevertheless, nothing can be done.

Such was the beginning of my acquaintance with my traveling companion, an acquaintance at first totally unproductive. Gradually, though, I was able to break through to something more fruitful, and to feel something more than cold curiosity for the man.

3

"I WAS SAVED by my game leg," my traveling companion continued when we were again seated opposite one another in the darkness. The night train had left Fastov's station behind in its little pool of brightness that lit up the sleepless cares of humankind like faces around a fire. Sleepy towns passed by the window, quiet villages cradled in slumber. But for us there could be no thought of sleep.

"It was being a cripple that saved me," he went on. "It meant I always had a stick with me. Not those fancy crutches you can buy nowadays at the pharmacy, good only for flicking dust off a jacket, the sort that would have broken if used on a Red Army peasant skull. No, it was with a proper hardwood stick that I cracked Grigory Chubinets on the forehead after he drunkenly got to his feet with the help of his one good arm. As he was falling to the ground, I cracked him a second time, landing one right on the old noggin, as they say. The bayonet he used for butchering people lay beside him. I grabbed it, both to defend myself and to prevent him from using it if he came to and caught up with me, which was not unlikely, because I, being a cripple, was slow. I realized I had to hide not only from Grigory but also from the authorities, who would consider me his partner in crime. Of course I was not really his partner, but I *had* helped carry human flesh around in sacks, though unwittingly. I knew it wasn't beef, of course, but had figured it couldn't be anything worse than dog or horse meat.

"All that night I sat in the concrete pit near the railway water tower, trying to work out a plan of escape. I had nowhere to turn, and people were starving all around me. The pit was freezing, colder than the storage sheds, but I thought nobody would suspect I was there. Yet somehow or other Grigory found me. Leaning over the edge of the pit, he stared at me calmly as I reached for the bayonet I had taken. For once he was stone-cold sober, and for once the rottenness was gone from his face. He regarded me with a look of compassion— whether for me or for himself, I don't know. A dark cloth was clumsily wrapped around his head, so that his pointed Red Army cap was cockeyed, sticking out over one ear.

" 'Come on out, Sasha, don't be afraid of me,' he said in the voice he had used when he visited us at home, bringing gifts for Aunt Steffie. 'Come on out of there, Sasha. I've written a note to a friend I served with in the Civil War. He's a big-shot commissar now. I was going to go see him myself, but I've run out of road now.'

"He spoke evenly, without hurrying, his tone of voice never changing, and I found myself believing what he said. I scrambled out of the pit, but kept a firm grip on the bayonet. Grigory looked at me and smiled. But it was only his lips that were smiling; his eyes were brimming with tears. I've seen a lot of smiles in my life, but only a few like that. It was the smile of a man who has said good-bye to this world but still, for some reason, finds himself alive, alive but longing for the grave.

" 'Why are you so clumsy with your stick, boy?' Grigory said at last. 'It's a fine stick. You should have whacked me across the bridge of my nose instead of on my forehead. Then, when I was on the ground, you shouldn't have hit me on the skull—the skull's too hard. The temple is softer—here, by the ear.'

"And with a gnarled finger he jabbed himself in the temple, so hard I was afraid he would burst his head open with his own finger, right before my eyes. Then he reached into his coat pocket and from it drew a grayish piece of newspaper that smelled of uncut tobacco. He handed it to me. In the margin he had written an address in a town not too far away, near Skvira but in the opposite direction from our home village, over toward Makhnovka and Polovetskoe.

" 'Leave as fast as you can,' he said. 'I'll help you hop a freight train. Leave while you're still alive. And if you see Steffie, give her a kiss from me, a good old-fashioned Red Army kiss. But let me have my bayonet back. You don't need it; it'll come in handy for me. . . . No, no, not for the old business. I need it for something different.'

"So I let him have his bayonet back, though I learned later that he didn't use it on himself. Instead, he hanged himself from the branch of an old oak in the stretch of forest where we had cooked and eaten human flesh together, and where in an alcoholic frenzy he had wanted to turn me into another rump steak. Now Grigory Chubinets was beyond the reach of human justice. The butcher and the cook were caught and executed by firing squad, but somehow I was left out, either because my track was cold or because the police weren't interested in chasing a runaway child."

The train wheels squealed and groaned, and the brakes hissed. We were suddenly jolted, and my companion's cane again fell to the floor.

"Stavishche," he said, glancing through the window. It was strange to hear the name of this place uttered in the same voice that had been used to tell of a man's participation in acts of cannibalism.

I bent down and picked up his cane, remembering how difficult it had been for him to do so the last time, how twisted his movements. He thanked me.

"How long is the stop here?" I asked.

"About five minutes," he said. "But you never can tell. Sometimes, if they're trying to make up time, the train stops for only two minutes. Let's wait till we reach Paripsy. We can get something to drink and take a short walk there."

And the train did start off again in a couple of minutes, with a sudden jerk that again knocked the cane to the floor. Again I picked it up.

36

"My cane's giving you trouble," he said. "I'd better hang it next to my beret."

"No, it'll be safer on the luggage rack, beside your briefcase," I said, and put it there. "Now it won't budge."

We traveled a considerable distance and were clattering across the ravine halfway between Stavishche and Boguiki, but my companion remained quiet. I thought his storytelling was over, that he had fallen asleep, and that I would have to sit listening to the clackety-clack of the wheels beneath the sleeping car instead of to his voice. I would hardly be able to sleep now. But Chubinets was not asleep; he was simply sitting with his eyes shut.

"I do not understand," he said finally, "how I was able to escape from the darkness I lived through into a brighter world, even if that brighter world was still pretty dismal. There I was, just a short while before, racked by bloody diarrhea and then an unwitting cannibal, and I'd barely escaped becoming a human meal myself. And now I was furious if I couldn't get tickets for a play at the local theater, or I lay on my bed and worried about how better to distribute lottery tickets for Osoviakhim. Or I worried because I wanted to win an encouraging smile from Galina Shchebivovk, the Young Communist League organizer at the soft-drinks plant where I had found a job. I think our life here on Earth is unnatural. We should trust neither our sorrows nor our joys. If we don't despair and don't rejoice, we have less trouble reconciling the blacks, the whites, the grays of life into a seamless whole. Life is a doormat at the gate to heaven; before entering paradise, everyone has to wipe his feet on it, saints and sinners alike.

"It turned out that Grigory's friend was not really a big-shot commissar, but he did find me a job as a drayman in a plant that made soft drinks and beer. I liked the work, and I knew how to handle the horses which pulled the flat wagons loaded with barrels or cases of bottles. My game leg was no great hindrance in this job.

"If you remember, it was the Age of Enthusiasm. In the films of those days, that was how people described it, and there were songs about it. The name was right too. I don't know about the older generation, but the young people in those years were always fired with enthusiasm. It was as if we had been put on a stove and heated; we boiled over like millet porridge when it's made without milk or fat and turns sticky. Once, an astronomer came from Kiev to give us a lecture, bringing a portable telescope with him. He would let you look at the sun through it for a ruble fifty. One ruble and fifty kopecks was then the price of an ice cream. I looked through the telescope, and the sun was like boiling millet porridge. Yes, in those days we looked at the world through a telescope, and everything we saw was boiling over.

"Besides working, I went to night school. By 1940 I had completed seven grades and was close to graduating. I was also in three amateur groups: a literary group organized by Saul Abramovich Bisk, who taught at the Nechui-Levitsky Teacher Training School; a drama group run by Leonid Pavlovich Semyonov, an actor at the local theater; and a group for political education, headed by Comrade Popach, a lecturer from the town party committee and chairman of the local branch of Osoviakhim. This Popach didn't have much education but spoke with great conviction. They say he couldn't tell the difference between a quote from Lenin and one from Molotov, but he was always up on the podium at formal occasions. He loved the words 'first principles,' though he pronounced big words like a provincial. He liked to call himself a pedagogue instead of a lecturer. Once, when he was beaten up in a bar, he shouted, 'How dare you strike a pedagogue!' As far as book learning was concerned, he and Saul Abramovich Bisk were like night and day, but they had similar temperaments. Bisk was really all fired up. Whenever he opened his mouth, words like 'Proletarian International,' 'Paris Commune,' 'opportunism,' 'Trotskyism,' and 'fascism' came pouring out.

"When Vojnicz's play *Ovod* was discussed at the Ivan Kocherga, our local theater, Bisk damned it. He claimed it portrayed a saccharine revolution. 'Our young people,' he said, 'do not need men like Charsky, who describe the Revolution in sentimental terms.' Charsky was a petit bourgeois antiproletarian writer. I must say, Bisk was always good to me, because of my underprivileged background, and he encouraged me in my first efforts at writing and advised me to read Kirshon's plays. Not everyone agreed with Bisk about *Ovod*, which Leonid Pavlovich Semyonov acted in. In fact, most people were against him, including me—particularly when Galina Shchebivovk spoke out in defense of the play. Like most girls in the town, she was in love with Leonid Pavlovich, which wasn't surprising, since he was a wonderful, openhearted individual and a talented actor—tall, and with a baritone voice and great charm. Despite all his opportunities with women, he lived alone with a blind sister who was much older than him. You can imagine how indignant many people were at Bisk's attack on Leonid Pavlovich. Galina Shchebivovk got right up and accused Bisk, to his face, of demagoguery, adding that she knew he was from the same town as Trotsky and even physically resembled him, what with his goatee and glasses. At these words the whole atmosphere in the theater changed. Bisk turned pale and left, and Leonid Pavlovich was given an ovation. Gladky, the director of the local theater, presented him with a bouquet of flowers, and Popach, the chairman of Osoviakhim, awarded him coupons for a new suit, declaring that the renowned actor had won it in the Osoviakhim lottery. The lottery, Popach went on to declare unnecessarily, was a totally voluntary activity conducted by the working people themselves, and everyone should buy tickets for the next drawing, which would take place in November 1941. What would happen to Popach and where he would be by then, nobody, of course, could have guessed.

"Among the people who influenced me in one way or another was an old man named Saltykov, who was chief librarian in the Saltykov-Shchedrin Library. He was an old-fashioned man, a former nobleman, and as such he had been disenfranchised—that is, he didn't have the right to vote in general elections. This old man, who wrinkled his nose at the very mention of Kirshon's name, was the first to tell me about such writers as Gogol and Dostoyevsky. Nowadays I read only newspapers, but in those days books kept me all fired up as well. Everything was new; there was a sense of discovery, of having one's eyes opened for the first time. I remember the excitement *Diary of an Idiot* brought me."

When I smiled at his mixing together Dostoyevsky and Gogol, he said, "Yes, an amusing book, but as I read it I wept as well as laughed. Look at me! I'm wiping my eyes even now, although I've long since forgotten what the book was about. It was as if reading it somehow put an end to my aversion to my family, freed me from the revulsion I felt for my evil brothers and sisters, for my mother, who was indifferent to me, and for my cruel father. Suddenly I was able to feel sorry for them and mourn them. Filled with gratitude to old Saltykov for all he'd taught me, I unburdened my soul to him. I told him I loved the theater but could never become an actor because I was a cripple, and so I wanted to be a playwright and, in fact, had already written one or two things. I told him I'd been encouraged to write by Saul Abramovich Bisk. Lord, Bisk's name rolled off my tongue like thunder, and at the sound of it, Saltykov's eyes flashed like lightning, and his face suddenly became young again. Hatred is always a youthful emotion.

" 'Soon their Judaic rule will end,' he pronounced, looking vaguely around, as if somebody else was speaking through his mouth. But nobody else was there, because it was a winter evening and we were walking across the frozen town park, an icy wind swirling around us, and it was so cold that not even the skating rink was open.

"Incidentally, our soft-drinks plant and brewery had reduced its output for the winter season, particularly the kvass and fruit drinks, but the beer too. Production had been cut by several thousand gallons, and part of the work force was assigned to other food-processing work. I had to sink cement pits for storing sauerkraut. I caught a bad cold doing it, ended up coughing my lungs out and running a high fever. Old Saltykov invited me to stay at his place, where his wife, Maria Nikolaevna, made me drink cup after cup of tea sweetened with stewed raspberries. They were good people, fired up like the rest of us but far less demonstrative about it. I told them my whole life story, though obviously only the part I had lived through until then. They were extremely sorry for me, and sometimes during my account they wrung their small, refined old hands, hands that belonged to the aristocrats they were, and they damned the oppressors. Maria Nikolaevna cursed the Jewish Bolsheviks, 'celebrating their Red Easter.' She asked me whether any of my family had survived, and when I told her that Aunt Steffie had left the village, she said I should write to her, in case she had gone back home. I thought about this for a while and decided that the Grigory Chubinets affair was over and done with. So I wrote to her. It turned out that she had indeed gone back home, and was working on the collective farm. She had repaired our old house out of her savings from the Urals, and she invited me to come visit her.

"When I arrived in Chubintsy, I found that the village

was alive once more, though with far fewer gardens, a pond choked with weeds, and a much smaller population. The village had not only been resuscitated but also was hard at work and inching its way back to some kind of self-sufficiency. The families of the hardest-working members of the collective-farm gangs had even managed to acquire windup phonographs and bicycles. Though I was just on vacation there, I sniffed around, and it smelled like home. The village was now run by the chairman of the collective farm, a former militiaman named Olekha Chubinets, a distant relative of ours. Steffie was being courted by his deputy, Mikola Chubinets, who, despite the name, was not related to us.

"One day Aunt Steffie, Mikola, and I were sitting around the table, drinking and eating fried pork rinds. After listening to my account of town life, Mikola said, 'Good for you! You're intelligent, you got ahead.'

"But when it was his turn to tell about the village, he spoke in a dull mechanical voice. 'The end justifies the means,' he said, then downed his glass of plum brandy, ate a pork rind, became red in the face, sniffed an onion, and added, in a sardonic, more human voice: 'But, as we say on the collective farm, it's the means that pay for the end. Everyone has an end of his own, so the most important thing is to get the means to pay for it.' "

4

AGAIN THE TRAIN gave a jerk, and from far away the buffers began to ring like metallic applause, a cold and hard, not a fleshy and warm, sound like hands clapping. The cars on our train were applauding our arrival in Boguiki, a minor stop on the Southwestern Railway. It was just an empty, poorly lighted platform, and the village beyond it consisted of wooden houses, whose inhabitants were sleeping lightly till dawn. A brief and gentle summer shower had ended moments before our arrival. Here and there the sound of dripping could still be heard, and the smell of damp turf, probably from the muddy flatcars standing on adjacent tracks, their canvas covers half slipping off, drifted through the window.

I looked out at Boguiki and then at my traveling companion, Sasha Chubinets. I was struck by the similarity between this village and this man. How easily the one could be taken for the other, I thought, and how easy it would be to get lost in either. What if, instead of continuing on my way, I went down now among those wooden houses, as you plunge into the depths of a forest? I had no need for Boguiki or for the Life and Hard Times of Sasha Chubinets. I was losing my beauty sleep on account of him, wasting time I could have spent reading Sophocles.

But the creative act requires that you give of yourself, to the last drop of blood, if need be. Listening to Chubinets meant letting him drink my blood. He was a vampire breathing life into the shadowy being he had been for me before I began listening to his story. That shadowy being receiving my blood was pulling me deeper and deeper into a world of gloom, where time and space were blurred and the living met the dead. There, Listener, Narrator, and Character constantly changed bodies, faces, and voices. How, I asked myself, could Chubinets recall his exact words and deeds after so many years, and remember who had done what or said what in each instance? And what gave him the ability to recall their individual thoughts, to evoke the way they looked or smiled? All this required the presence of a Listener, someone to contribute the lifeblood of his own memory. But the Listener/victim, even as he yielded up his blood to the Narrator/vampire, was not purely passive. No. Because the divine spark does not lie in creativity. The bringing of being out of nothingness, the creation of something new, that is not what is holy. The holiness is, rather, in loving what has already been created. And that love embraces both genius and mediocrity, both Sophocles and Sasha Chubinets, and makes Boguiki's dark wooden houses the equal of the grand palaces of Venice.

"We've been held up here too long," said Sasha Chubinets, looking at the illuminated dial of his wristwatch. "Now the Paripsy signalmen will not let the train stay in their sector, and we won't have much time to go to the well there. The water in that well is wonderfully pure."

So he didn't want only my blood; he wanted fresh spring water too. Yes, there really was something unpleasantly vampirelike about this man. I considered the possibility of turning my back on him, thereby returning him to his shadowy status. But I had already put too much of myself into this Ukrainian Byron, this Gypsy baron, this lame lyricist with musical-comedy ideas.

"Three things led me to write a play," said Chubinets, resuming his tale. "First, the books I had read on old Saltykov's recommendation. Second, the visit to our town by a well-known Moscow theater company. And third, the fact that I fell in love. Yes, I was in love; and a strange love it was too. But then again, what love isn't strange? Do you remember that popular song at the time about blue eyes and golden curls? The one that went like this."

And he sang, in a pleasant baritone:

> *"Your deep blue eyes and golden curls*
> *That marked you out from other girls*
> *The trees along the avenue*
> *And station yard still speak of you. . . ."*

He crooned rather than sang, to the clicking of the wheels as our train neared the wonderful well in Paripsy. His singing cheered me up, and I prepared myself to hear something more pleasant than tales of human meat and garlic.

"The company from Moscow played at the Kocherga theater, and through Leonid Pavlovich Semyonov I got tickets for two of its productions. One was a play called *Rust*, and the other was *Natalya Tarpova*. The two plays had such an impact on me that, for the first time, I formed an opinion independent of either Saltykov or Bisk. In fact, Bisk and I actually quarreled over the plays. He didn't like them, particularly *Rust*, and felt that the company was using a Soviet proletarian play to make an anti-Soviet statement. *Natalya Tarpova* he dismissed as petty-bourgeois theater. He was more reticent in public, but revealed his true opinions to me at the dinner table, where we would argue questions of aesthetics between bites of gefilte fish cooked by his wife, Fanny Abramovna. After Galina Shchebivovk accused him of being a Trotskyite, Bisk had become more circumspect, and thus had been less specific, during the public discussion of the two plays. He supported a Soviet theater based on class lines and run by proletarian playwrights.

"I was listening to what he had to say with less interest than before—indeed, I also listened with less interest to what those who disagreed with him had to say. Because when a man forms his own ideas, he's bored by the ideas of others. Suddenly the producer from Moscow began to speak. I think he was a Tatar—at least, that's what he looked like. His words—and this was the first time this ever happened—impressed me the way some of Gogol's sentences do. What he said was: 'Life must be regarded with a misty and joyous eye.' I was bowled over by the beauty of this phrase, and envious of him for saying it, for being capable of thinking it up. For the first time in my life I felt the pangs of vanity and of envy of someone else's knowledge. Such emotions are the handmaidens of creativity. And so it was, what with the discussion of the plays and my new vanity, that I seized my courage with both hands and opened my mouth to ask the Tatar a challenging question.

" 'You say,' I said, perspiring profusely in my excitement, 'a misty and joyous eye. But what precisely does this mean? Dialectically speaking, it is not one misty and joyous eye that we must have, but two. . . .'

"Misty eyes indeed! Mine had become so fogged over as I spoke that it was like looking at the Tatar through a cloud. The whole audience tittered at my question, and that was my answer. The Tatar laughed too, but he alone realized that I was tongue-tied, and he seemed to sympathize entirely with my agitation. After the discussion, he singled me out from other admirers surrounding him and invited me to his hotel, where for the first time in my life I drank green tea and ate sweet dried apricots. And for the first time I saw a woman who . . . but it is beyond my power to describe her. She was his wife and an actress, and I not only saw her, but also talked with her, and answered her when she spoke to me. All the time we were together, I was surprised that she was a living being like the rest of humankind, which meant that she did everything a living person did. I even felt offended that she smelled of perfume rather than being of odorless marble. And with these thoughts, it suddenly dawned on me why it was the Tatar, and not me, who had invented the phrase about the misty and joyous eye.

"During the hour or so I spent with them, they asked me about myself, and I told them about the village of Chubintsy and my dead family. But I restrained myself and didn't mention the part about the human flesh. I told them that I loved the theater, and that since I was a cripple and couldn't act, I wanted to write plays. The Tatar was very encouraging and asked his wife to write down the address of their theater so that I could send my plays there. I watched her tear a sheet of paper from a notepad and write out the address, knowing that a minute earlier I might have crumpled up this sheet of paper, torn it into pieces, and thrown it into the trash without a second thought. But now I carefully folded it and put it away in a safe place.

"From then on, I began looking for a woman like the Tatar's wife to love. Of course this was outright gall on my part—I, a Ukrainian peasant, a cripple, and a drayman at a soft-drinks plant! But I was already being consumed by the vanity that Saul Abramovich Bisk and old Saltykov, in their different ways, had kindled in me. Through Leonid Pavlovich Semyonov, I saw the Tatar's wife twice more, though at a distance: once while she was giving a class on makeup to the actors at the theater, and again when she delivered a talk on the fundamentals of drama. As long as she was in town, I didn't dare look at another woman, of course. But I began looking as soon as she left. For a while I hung around Galina Shchebivovk, but whenever she came to the soft-drinks plant, she kept her white Persian-silk stockings as far away as possible from my sticky overalls and their fruity stench. Then I discovered she had a lover, who was in charge of fencing and self-defense courses run by Osoviakhim. Because of Grigory Chubinets, anything to do with blades and fighting aroused a great repugnance in me, and after a while Galina herself became less attractive for the same reason. At meetings, when she came out with statements like 'We Soviet patriots, fiancées, sisters, and wives, are prepared, if we should be called, to go out into the fields, into the factories, and to the front, to keep the enemy's claws off our towns and settlements,' I had an overwhelming desire to tell her that I had dined on human flesh barbecued on a bayonet.

"Although any woman, of course, paled in comparison with the Tatar's wife, I nonetheless did finally catch sight of one who resembled her. A remote resemblance, as that popular song about deep blue eyes remotely resembled an immortal aria. Once, at the train station, I happened to see a young woman step down to the platform. She held a bunch of pink Crimean grapes in one hand and was plucking them off and popping them into her mouth with the other. Everything about her reminded me of the song with the golden curls and deep blue eyes. The whistle soon sounded, and she climbed back onto the train, her shapely legs and little sandals vanishing forever as the train pulled out. But I never forgot her. As I said, she had something in common with the Tatar's wife, this girl on the Simferopol train. Her image constantly before me, I began writing the play *A Ruble and Two Bits*, about the love of a cripple for a beautiful young woman.

"I wrote it in the evenings and on my days off, in my basement room, which I had been allocated as a reward for good work at the plant. When the play was finished, I carefully copied it out. Then, for a modest fee, Saul Abramovich arranged for it to be typed in duplicate on an Underwood. He kept one copy to read himself, and I sent the other to the address in Moscow that the Tatar's wife had written down for me. From then on, the mailbox played a key role in my life—one of those regulation dark blue boxes sometimes mistaken by country people for outgoing mail, particularly when they are hanging outside, rather than in a hallway. Ours was in the lobby.

"Waiting for a reply was a new and disturbing experience, and my life began to hang on that single thread. If my play was accepted, I would be a successful peasant writer, like Esenin, although I must say I didn't much care for his poetry. After agonizing months of expectation, during which I suffered from headaches and insomnia, I found that rejection slip in the mailbox, at five in the morning, on June 22, 1941, as I said previously.

"A week earlier, I had caught a cold, had been coughing till I practically suffocated, and was feeling very weak and running a high temperature. My hands trembled, and one day I dropped a case of raspberry juice while trying to load it. The bottles broke; I was reprimanded and had to pay for the whole case out of my wages.

Then, after that, I was late for work. But because I had a reputation as a hard worker who wasn't in the habit of doing things sloppily, I wasn't docked for lateness. Instead, they gave me a medical certificate and put me on sick leave starting June 17. I went straight to Chubintsy to see Aunt Steffie and recuperate. I got better quickly and even went fishing a couple of times with Mikola Chubinets, who was now my aunt's husband. But I was impatient, and turning down the chance to go fishing on June 22, I left for town the evening before. And so I found the rejection slip from the theater. It wasn't signed by the Tatar or his wife, but by somebody I'd never heard of. I'd curse him now, but can't remember his name. After ripping the envelope open and reading the slip by the midsummer dawn's half-light there in the lobby, I went down to my basement room, slammed the door, locked myself in, and pulled the shutters closed. Then I got into bed and went to sleep.

"It was hard to tell whether I was asleep or simply daydreaming, and I don't know how much time went by. I vaguely remember hearing the noise of many people passing my cellar window, the roar of engines, the clatter of hooves, thunder from a storm, and probably the patter of raindrops. Several times people knocked on my door, but they went away when there was no reply. In my mind, all this noise and turmoil was somehow connected with the rejection of my play. Things went on like this for two or three days.

"Thirsty, I drank a lot of water, which I kept in bottles. I sometimes brought home raspberry drink or seltzer or bread beer, which I preferred to the regular kind, from the plant, and so I had lots of empty bottles. Since the water from my basement tap always had sand in it, I always filled the bottles and let the sand settle before I drank. And I corked the bottles tightly to keep the water fresh. Once, I wasn't just thirsty but hungry too, and I reached for a stale piece of bread that was lying on the table. Instead of biting off a hunk of the bread, I accidentally bit my finger. It hurt terribly, and I was horrified at the sight of the foxlike tooth marks on my wounded finger and of the blood on the bread. I cried out, thinking that I was hallucinating, but managed to pull myself together.

"Soon after, there was thunder again outside, and people screaming. My cellar walls shook like cardboard. I heard a knock on the door—it was boots, not fists, making the noise—accompanied by shouts for me to open up. I could hear children crying and women screaming and smelled smoke and quicklime. A desperate crowd came pouring into my room looking as if they were trying to hide from something. I knew only a few faces. One man was shouting desperately. It was Comrade Popach, chairman of Osoviakhim, wearing a white soldier's vest stuffed into riding breeches and brandishing a revolver.

" 'Deserter!' he was shouting. 'Lying here just waiting for the Germans to arrive, and stocked up with water! Let me tell you: Don't count the Soviets out yet!'

"I realized that this was reality, not a product of my hallucinating mind, and saw clearly that Popach was close to shooting me. I was scared to death, since I was young and eager to live.

" 'Comrade Popach!' I screamed too, because in a hysterical crowd there was little to be gained by talking in an ordinary voice. 'Comrade Popach! I'm a cripple!'

" 'Water! Water! We're thirsty!' several children yelled all at once.

" 'The town water mains have been blown up, and here he is hoarding water!' Popach shouted. 'You damned fascist! As soon as the all-clear sounds, I'm taking you to army headquarters!'

"With these words, he shoved his pistol back into its holster, seized one of my bottles, and tried to open it by smacking its base with his palm. I tried to tell him that you can't open bottles with rubber caps like that, but it was too late: the bottle burst in his hands. Wicked-looking shards of thick green glass embedded themselves in both his palms, and blood spurted onto the table and floor. Popach took one look and fainted. He was picked up by a woman railway sweeper and hauled away for first aid. Given my ordeal over the past few days and what was happening now right before my eyes, the news that war with Germany had been declared, that it was into its fifth day, and that the Germans were bombing the town came as no great surprise to me.

"For me, the war began on June 28, after I'd recovered from the shock of my literary rebuff. The bombing that day was particularly fierce, because Soviet army troops were retreating through the town. Since the bomb shelters were full, the people were taking refuge in the cellars of houses. I don't know how Popach happened to be among them, and without his combat gear too, though he was chairman of Osoviakhim, and had taught us how to be vigilant and prepared for war, with lectures on subjects like fire fighting during bombing raids. Apparently, the moment war broke out, his pupils had lost their nerve and run like rabbits to the cellars with everyone else, leaving the town defenseless. To my way of thinking at that point, after the collapse of my dreams, the condition of the town seemed completely appropriate. In fact, I would have been surprised if I had emerged from my five days of torment and not found sidewalks strewn with broken glass, tangles of wire hanging from telegraph poles, and trees, ripped up by their roots, lying on the streetcar tracks. I felt at home, a cripple in a crippled world.

"The first thing to do was get my affairs in order. I set off on foot to pick up my wages, since no streetcars were running to the soft-drinks plant. When I arrived, the building looked abandoned. The hand of bureaucratic authority had released the strings; and not just factories and companies but the entire town had collapsed in a heap, like a helpless rag puppet. Wherever you turned, something gaped at you, empty or shattered or scattered all over the place. One exception was the barbershop in the town park, or, more precisely, the exception was Lyova the barber, whom I used to go to occasionally for a shave. Of all the Jews in the town, I think he was the most mercenary, and the stupidest. Deciding to take advantage of the flight of his competitors, he intended, it seemed clear, to open his own barbershop as soon as the Germans arrived. He remembered the Germans who had come to the Ukraine in 1918, remembered them as a polite and cultured people.

Things had been safe during their occupation. Why Lyova was not afraid that I would denounce him to the NKVD, I don't know. Probably he was aware that the town's NKVD committee had already fled. Like all barbers, he was well informed, and, as he shaved me and cut my hair, he filled me in on what had happened over the last two days.

" 'There's no water in town because they bombed the water mains on Gogol Street. As many as two hundred people have been killed by bombs. They're court-martialing people for breaking blackout regulations—tenants and owners both. Some have been fined. One of my regulars, Levin the mechanic from the streetcar depot, was fined. He turned on his lights, opened his shutters, locked his apartment, and took off.' Here Lyova sniggered, as if it was a big joke. 'Another of my clients,' he continued, spraying cheap eau de cologne on me and cheering me up with his fatuous gossip, 'Fomin, the cashier from the medical school, got three months for being out after nine P.M. Despite the curfew, he went to see his girlfriend, a medical student.'

"Poor old Lyova. On July 3, one week later, the Germans were already on us. Not the Kaiser's Germans, but Hitler's; and we all found out what they were like, Lyova included. I met other people who were happy amid the general gloom and chaos: old Saltykov and his wife, Maria Nikolaevna. They were at the town library, the only ones there, sorting books, hurling the red, maroon, and deep-blue volumes of Marx, Engels, Lenin, and Stalin from the shelves. Mayakovsky and the other proletarian poets and writers all landed in that heap. So

Pushkin, Turgenev, Gogol, and Dostoyevsky got plenty of extra room and were able to make themselves more comfortable on the shelves. Old Saltykov too was waiting for the Germans, but his hopes were political, not economic, like those of Lyova.

" 'Congratulations,' he said to me. 'Congratulations on shaking off the yoke of the Jewish Communist International. Sasha, you are a young Russian, and soon you will once again be master in your own land, the Land of All the Russias.'

" 'You're looking poorly,' said his wife. 'What's wrong? Have you been ill?'

"I told them what had happened to me—not telling just them, but telling myself as well—and as I spoke, I recalled things I had ignored before because of the confusion. For example, that I no longer had a copy of *A Ruble and Two Bits*. After putting my entire soul into it, I had lost my last copy. In my ignorance and inexperience, I'd torn up the original draft after copying it, feeling somehow that, since it was the culmination of all my endeavors, of everything I had never had and everything that had caused me pain, it should not survive as a rough draft. But the copy was still with the typist, with whom I didn't have any contact, since Bisk had dealt with her directly. The typewritten copy I sent to the theater had probably been dumped in the trash, and Bisk had the other copy.

" 'On the other hand,' I said, 'if my play wasn't good enough for such well-known and clever people, perhaps I shouldn't bother about it.'

"The old man was furious at this story and at my

defeatism. He shouted at me, ordered me to go immediately to Bisk and get my play back before Bisk took off for Birobidzhan. He spoke about Bisk with a kind of mocking hatred and angry satisfaction, while Maria mimicked Fanny, Bisk's wife. Grimacing, puckering her lips, making her eyes bug out, she turned herself from a Russian lady who admired Turgenev into an old hag with twisted features as she imitated Fanny saying, 'Saul, Saul, you must eat your jam. . . .'

Taking advantage of a pause in Chubinets's narrative, I had a long swallow of Fastov water from my thermos. Chubinets turned to the window and looked out at the dark landscape racing past. Then the train emerged from clouds and drizzle; the moon shone brightly, and the car was bathed in white light. Chubinets too seemed to glow, and he turned playful. His thoughts, his images, his words became brighter. Where, I wondered, does the spirit of the Narrator end and that of his Listener begin? Because in the creation of a narrative, two hearts beat as one. No, I would not dissociate myself from a man who between Stavishche and Boguiki had confused Gogol and Dostoyevsky. Who is more important, the one who prospects for diamonds or the one who fashions them into pieces of jewelry and cuts them into gems? A foolish question, because the image of the blood-soaked bread when Chubinets bit his finger is mine, while the philosophizing is Chubinets's. Because he and I are one.

Chubinets continued: "There were high hopes in those first few days, weeks, months of the war among the inhabitants of the western Ukraine, hopes that things would change for the better, wild dreams that the world would be made new.

" 'You know what I dream of?' old Saltykov said to me after his wife's impersonation of Fanny Bisk. 'I dream of starting up a local Russian newspaper and using the word *Yid*. Not *Bundist* or *Zionist*, just the word *Yid*. The last time I had the pleasure of seeing that word in print was more than twenty years ago.'

"With this, he grabbed a balalaika from behind a shelf of books, plunked himself down on a chair, and with softened features, his head resting on his shoulder, began playing 'The moon shone bright, the moon shone bright . . .'

" 'The full moon shone bright,' Maria Nikolaevna joined in. 'Maria, Daria, and Vaselka all came dancing here.' She began tapping her foot, as if she was about to dance like a young girl.

" 'You know,' said Saltykov, continuing to strum, 'when I was a student at Saint Vladimir's University in Kiev, I used to play in a string band at a restaurant in order to earn a little money. Those were youthful, happy times. And we can bring them back. It's now up to you and me, Russians, to retie the knot undone by Jewish Bolshevism. In 1921, I tried to escape to go to Europe, but now Europe is coming to us, on German tanks.'

"He went on in this vein for a long time, jumping from one subject to another, but every subject was joyous and concerned with the rebirth of Russia. Then he came back to his normal self, looked at his pocket watch, and sent me off to see Bisk.

" 'And don't come back without your script,' he shouted after me.

"But I wasn't able to get in to see Bisk. Without opening the door, his maid, an old Ukrainian woman, said that her master was not home. I explained why I'd come, but she refused to let me in and told me to return the next morning. When I showed up bright and early, she informed me, again without unlocking the door, that her master had been evacuated.

" 'What do you mean, evacuated?' I asked.

" 'He's gone away,' she replied.

" 'Where to?'

" 'I don't know.'

" 'When did he leave?'

" 'He left for the station three hours ago.'

"Almost in tears, I raced through the ravaged town to the station, cursing Bisk in almost the same terms that old Saltykov had used. The station was packed, even though the ticket offices weren't open. Despite the bombardments, the building was still intact. The Germans wouldn't flatten it until 1944, when they were being pushed back and were trying to stave off the Soviet advance by bombing. I ran through the station to the platform, then jumped down and began running along the tracks, to catch the train that was carrying Bisk away with my play to Tashkent or God knows where. Why I thought Bisk would bother to take my play with him, as if it had some value, I don't know; probably it was because old Saltykov had got me thinking of it again as a great treasure. Troop trains and hospital cars stood on sidings and in the train yards, but nobody stopped me, since there was a swarm of people with suitcases and bundles racing in all directions. Children were crying; there was cursing and shouting. It was strange that in this confusion Bisk himself noticed me, and stranger yet that I heard his voice over the din.

" 'Sasha Chubinets!' he roared.

"He was sitting on a block of iron on a flatcar, all but squashed by other people with their bundles and suitcases in the midst of lathes and power tools, undoubtedly from a factory in the process of evacuation. Next to him was Fanny Abramovna, in a housecoat. They were obviously most uncomfortable, but they were holding on for dear life to the places they had managed to get by arriving at dawn.

" 'We've been waiting for four hours and haven't moved an inch,' Bisk complained, then he asked me for water. I brought them some in an aluminum flask he'd handed to me, and they both drank thirstily. I had just told him about my play and asked him for my copy when panic suddenly set in. Planes appeared above the station—and they had to be German planes, because they had command of the air by then, and our airfield was nothing but rubble. The chickenhearted shrill of locomotive whistles at this moment served to increase the panic. On the roof of a freight car in a nearby troop train, soldiers began aiming an antiaircraft gun on a high tripod.

" 'What are they doing, trying to fire at the planes?' Fanny Abramovna cried nervously. 'If they start firing, the planes will shoot back and hit *us!*'

"Her eyes were flashing maniacally, and her hair was

disheveled. I asked again about my play. Then all of a sudden the flatcar jerked forward, and they began to move. They were ecstatic.

" 'Your play is in the top drawer of my desk,' Bisk shouted, by way of farewell.

"It was not so easy to get at his desk, however. The old Ukrainian woman refused to open the door and told me to come back when her master returned. I complained to old Saltykov, who volunteered to help me, in part because he wanted to have a look at Bisk's books, with a view to appropriating any valuable editions. The town in the meantime had taken on an air of desperate festivity, such as children display when they are left unwatched. Shops and apartments abandoned by their owners, Jews for the most part, were looted. That was how we came to find the door to Bisk's apartment open, and the old maidservant weeping on the staircase. She asked us to call the militia, but old Saltykov looked at her gaily and cried, 'The days of Soviet rule are over.'

"Bisk's apartment had been ransacked, and what hadn't been taken had been smashed to bits. The floor was littered with papers, books, and fragments of an expensive mirror for which there had evidently been no room on the looters' cart. I found my play, not in the drawer of the mahogany writing desk, which had been gashed by ax blows, but crumpled, though complete, under a heap of books. Once more I had been lucky.

"Speaking of luck and good fortune, I had been curious after seeing the blue-eyed passenger on the Simferopol express to know what would happen to me in the long run, what the future held in store. Like a young lover who believes in the stars, I found a fortune-teller, one of those who say 'I'm not a Gypsy, I'm a Serb,' because Gypsies lie, but a Serbian woman can always be trusted. My Serbian woman predicted that being a cripple would bring me nothing but grief in my ordinary life, but it would be my salvation in difficult times. Turning over the cards, she said I should not fear the prison house or long journeys. There are games of chance that aren't worth the candle, and some that *are* worth it, and there is a game in which people turn into candles, burning themselves out or just guttering until they're a horrible, disgusting stub, of no use to anyone."

5

"THE FIRST THING the German-occupation authorities did when they arrived was to prohibit all males from leaving the town. Any attempt to do so meant concentration camp or firing squad. Since I had absolutely nothing to live on in town, somehow or other I had to get to Chubintsy. Although life soon became easier, and we were even able to use Soviet currency to buy sugar, milk, salt pork, meat, and vegetables at the market, I didn't have Soviet rubles, let alone German money. Those with jobs received ration cards that could be used for buying bread, buckwheat, salt, and sunflower oil (half a liter per month). But I didn't have a job. I wasn't hired for clerical work, couldn't find work as a drayman, and wasn't suited for heavy manual labor.

"I went to see old Saltykov, who was working for the municipal administration under the Ukrainian mayor, and he helped me obtain a pass to leave town. He also told me that plans were afoot to set up a theater in town, to stage musicals and dramas. He said that as soon as I revised my play to suit the New Order, I should present it in person to the theater director, the same Gladky who had been in charge before the German occupation. This was good news, and I learned that Leonid Pavlovich Semyonov had stayed behind too and would be in the theater company. I dreamed of having Leonid Pavlovich play the lead role in my play.

"In Chubintsy, as everywhere else in the country, the change of regime had been welcomed. When I arrived, having hitched a ride on a German truck, I learned that the changes had begun with the looting of Soviet property. Aunt Steffie told me that by the time she reached the village shop, all that was left were buttons and empty cardboard boxes. Villagers had taken the collective-farm property as well, carrying off animals, grain, and agricultural equipment. Immediately after this, however, the first dark cloud appeared on the horizon: the Germans had no intention of breaking up the collective and state farms; they simply changed their name to 'agricultural cooperatives' and left them as they were. The Kirov and the Komsomol Central Committee Collective Farms, as the two in our village were called, were rechristened the Chubintsy Agricultural Cooperative and divided into two teams. The collective-farm council was replaced by the village general council. In some villages, new chairmen were elected; in others, the original chairmen were left in place. In Chubintsy, the council meeting was attended by a German and the mayor of the chief town of the district, who were visiting us. The interpreter for the occasion was Dubok, who before the German invasion had been secretary to the Young Communist League, but was now in the German occupation's police force, the Polizei.

" 'Heil Hitler!' Dubok shouted as soon as the meeting began, jabbing out his right arm.

" 'Hi, Hitler,' the peasants, including Aunt Steffie, said in unison, and many thought: Maybe things will be better under Hitler.

"Our new leaders recommended that a Mr. Chubinets be selected as chairman, but since more than half the village was named Chubinets, they had to be more precise. So they named a certain Olekha Chubinets. This was the same Olekha Chubinets who had been in charge of the collective farm before the Germans arrived. But he wanted no part of the job, afraid that when our people returned, he would be jailed. Which, as it turned out, is what happened, although his wife was allowed to keep the Soviet medals he had received. At first she kept them locked up in the collective-farm safe, but later she buried them.

"Gradually, the elation of the first few months of the German occupation gave way to the fear that the Soviets would come back and make us pay for our pleasure. Actually, though, it was the Germans who began to make us pay. They had us get up at the crack of dawn to weed beets. Weeding is always a rushed and hectic affair with us, because of the weather. Fall is dry and warm, and even though by the beginning of November the low clouds of winter still haven't set in, there's always the danger of an early frost, which can quickly ruin the beet and potato harvest. We generally have adequate rainfall in the summer, but not really as much in the autumn as the winter crops need. A German agronomist was dispatched to the village to deal with such problems; he strode around the fields with Olekha Chubinets and sat in the boardroom of the village cooperative. It was decided, reasonably enough, to abolish the whole complicated Soviet system of resolutions, orders, work days, and awards to faster workers and replace it with a simple solution: a German overseer with a bullwhip. The German selected for the job was a brute and, worse, didn't know a single word of Russian or Ukrainian. Since he didn't understand a thing, he would whip you at the slightest provocation. Where the Soviet commissars would have first issued a reprimand, the German just used his whip. One time, Aunt Steffie came back with a long welt across her back.

" 'What did you get that for?' I asked.

" 'For wearing my red dress to work,' she said.

"Later, my own back was to bear the marks of the new approach, as did the backs of others. Any German had the right to strike anyone from the village, for any reason. He could beat the villagers, maim them, even kill them, and nothing would happen to him, because there was no one to complain to. Aunt Steffie, however, had no intention of complaining, since she had a Soviet soldier hidden in her cellar. Mikola Chubinets, her husband, had been drafted into the Red Army on the second day of the war, and his whereabouts were unknown.

"The front had not taken long to pass through Chubintsy, but for quite a while thereafter stragglers from the Red Army would pass through the village by ones and twos. The man at Aunt Steffie's had an arm wound that refused to heal, although she kept applying poultices to it. He couldn't bear sitting around doing nothing and started making oil lamps out of bottles, which Aunt Steffie would trade for food. In the smoky light of these lamps, I spent my evenings rewriting *A Ruble and Two Bits*. During the day, I drove carts for the cooperative with another disabled individual, Vanya Chubinets, who was walleyed and a little queer in the head. The children would shout 'Ruble and Two Bits' at me and call 'Squinty, Squinty!' after him. Clearly, Vanya and I were meant to be buddies. Anyway, the work wasn't too bad at first: carting rotten beets and potatoes to the pig farm, mucking the pens, and spreading the manure on the kitchen gardens. We did all the work ourselves. I had not forgotten how to use a pitchfork and spade, farm boy that I was. On one occasion we received an order from the cooperative management to make two trips out to the pig farm, but then had to make a third run out toward the village of Krivosheintsy and unload at the brickworks there.

" 'Why take spoiled beets and rotten cabbage out to the brickworks when it isn't operating anymore?' I wondered out loud. 'It's a fourteen-kilometer round trip. Why wear out the horse by going so far?'

" 'You'll see why when you get there,' replied Olekha Chubinets, obviously none too happy about the reason. But what choice did he have? Like us, he was not free. Orders are orders.

"So we drove the cart out to Krivosheintsy, and there we saw Germans and Polizei, and barbed wire strung around the outside of the brickworks. We drove in through the gates and got a whiff of something awful. Immediately, memories of collectivization came flooding back, visions of men dying in front of each other as routinely as, in normal times, they would have gone on living. I recalled the indescribable stink of black diarrhea and blood, and the pinkish color of mucusy vomit.

"When I was inside the gates, I saw a dark crowd behind another barbed-wire fence. They all seemed to be dressed in black, the grown-ups and the children, of which there were many. Actually, they weren't all dressed the same, but their surroundings worked on them like an optical illusion, clothing them in black, as if a huge flock of adult and fledgling crows was weakly fluttering about in a heap after being shot down out of the sky—still alive but waiting to be finished off.

"Now, I happen to like crows. They're intelligent birds, and know better than to trust human beings, even though they live alongside them. And there I was looking at the Germans and at our Ukrainian Polizei, while behind this second fence of barbed wire I saw, in my imagination, a flock of wounded crows violently thrown out of the trees.

" 'Unload, Chubinets,' shouted Dubok, who was

there too. 'Chuck the feed at them. These Yids can't have fried chicken every day of the week. During collectivization, did they care about us while we were dying? No, they were in town living off the fat of the land. They had ration books, the bastards.'

"So we forked the slimy beets and rotten potatoes over the barbed-wire fence, and the Jews threw themselves on the stuff and began to chew it on the spot, or tried to grab it from one another. Some of the Germans laughed; others turned away in scorn, muttering, '*Jü-dische Schweine.*'

"I don't know why those local Jews were kept alive at the brickworks. I suppose general instructions still hadn't been issued, that the special plan for exterminating the Jewish nation still hadn't been devised. As a result, in different localities the Germans did different things.

"Incidentally, much later, during rehearsals for my play, *A Ruble and Two Bits*, I met an actor named Pasternakov. Not Pasternak, the famous poet. This one was a well-known comic actor from Odessa, who appeared in lots of Soviet films, as a shock worker, a tractor driver, a pilot, and so on. Maybe that was why he had problems with the Germans after Odessa was taken. He had been decorated under Soviet rule, had been a deputy to the Soviet municipal council in Odessa, but under the Germans had been in a labor camp. Finally, he was released and came to work in our theater. He couldn't really display his talents with us, since he appeared only in crowd scenes and did walk-ons, but even for that he had reason to be grateful, because it was very difficult to get work in theaters.

"Since theater people were not mobilized to work in Germany, many young men and women tried to get jobs with the company, begging for any work and agreeing to anything to avoid being sent into enemy territory. Moreover, a theater ticket for local people cost only three rubles, whereas a loaf of bread at the market cost two hundred, but everyone on the theater payroll received first-class rations and passes permitting them to stay out after curfew. The Germans also patronized the theater and paid for their tickets in ostmarks, one of which was the equivalent of ten rubles. Actors averaged a salary of one thousand three hundred rubles a month. Leonid Pavlovich was the only one to get a fixed salary, two thousand rubles, the same salary as Gladky, the director and chief producer. Ivan Semyonovich Czech, who was always Leonid Pavlovich's rival, under both the Soviet regime and the German occupation, received one thousand five hundred. A change in regime doesn't alter people or add to their talents. Lelya Romanova, a beautiful young actress with a fine voice who played the leading ladies, also received one thousand five hundred. Her husband was a pilot in the Soviet air force, but she was now going out with Germans, and she had a German officer as a boarder.

"Pasternakov, despite his former fame in Odessa, received only eight hundred rubles. Thanks to his time in a German labor camp, he also had a suppurating wound in his arm, and the only thing that kept him from going under was his professional skill and his comical looks. He had a habit of making wisecracks, though. When *A Ruble and Two Bits* was in rehearsal, he had the part of Gryts Tsybuli, the hero's best friend, which he performed wonderfully. Once, after a rehearsal, I asked him about his arm and how he came to be injured, because I wanted to tell him how Aunt Steffie had treated her injured soldier's wound.

" 'I burned it on a Jew,' Pasternakov replied.

"He's joking, I thought, expecting the usual funny story.

" 'It's true,' he said. 'The Germans took Odessa on October 17, 1941. The next day, posters were put up requiring all Jews in Odessa and outlying areas to report for registration at the flying school on the airfield out on Lüstdorf Road. On the morning of October 19, the people of Odessa saw crowds of Jews of all ages, from very old to very young, walking down Lüstdorf Road, because anyone who didn't register would be shot. I know the place well—I played the part of an airman there before the war, in a film for Odessa Film Studios, and in May 1941, just before the war began, I took part in a concert there for student pilots. The flying school was next to enormous warehouses, used as ammunition dumps, nine of them in all. German soldiers herded the Jews into the warehouses, then used pumps and hoses to spray everything with a fuel mixture and burn the people alive. The screams, the flames, and the horrible smell of burning bodies kept everyone awake that night, even those who lived some distance from the airfield.

The screams were the first things to fade away, and then the flames, but the stench hung over the place for weeks.' "

With these words, Pasternakov fell silent—or, rather, Chubinets fell silent. And in my role as Listener, I too was silent. We were traveling through the countryside on a mail train in the depths of the Ukrainian night, with a brilliant moonlit sky visible through the windows. The moon silvered everything it touched: the tracks, objects along the embankment, the galvanized roofs of the sturdier houses, and from time to time the water in small lakes and streams. Everything glistened. On moonlit nights in the Ukraine, it's unusually calm, reassuring, free of menace. Chubinets and I breathed more easily, relaxing in the moonlight as if, after a long scramble up a cliff face, we had suddenly found ourselves resting in a dry cave.

"Pasternakov told me about the stink of cooked human flesh," Chubinets continued, "and I recalled the same odor from my experience during the famine. The Germans were not yet eating human flesh, admittedly. But if Hitler managed to conquer the world, who knows what they might do? Not out of starvation, as we did in 1934, but because they had turned into beasts. The victorious German with bullwhip and submachine gun was a completely different species, believe me, from today's mild German tourist with his Zeiss camera. Everyone had to give way to our German masters, and if men didn't tip their caps to them, they were struck across the face. That was what happened to Leonid Pavlovich Semyonov, even though he was a well-known actor, and, much earlier, to me.

"Once, because of my bad leg, I stumbled and accidentally stepped on a German officer's foot. My God, you wouldn't believe the beating he gave me. He didn't just hit me; he pounded me, smashing my face and kicking me in the stomach. Broke my nose. He was obviously very annoyed about something. Imagine a healthy young ox of a soldier beating the living daylights out of a cripple in front of everyone. At least the Soviet authorities, if they knocked us around, did so in the privacy of their offices or down in a cellar, for appearance's sake or out of common decency. But when the Germans started feeling like lords of creation, they became utterly shameless. They would emit these huge farts if nobody but Ukrainians was around, and in the countryside they'd piss and shit right in front of the women. Obviously, not all of them were like this. But I can't recall one German ever reprimanding another for that kind of thing. I don't think the German authorities ever punished any of their own for looting—or, for that matter, murder.

"The first few months of the summer, they were still bearable, and would come and draw pictures of chickens in the sand and pay in ostmarks for milk and eggs. But by the time winter came, they had turned into savages. They would gun down chickens, for example, with their automatic weapons. On one occasion, a German was killed at a Chubintsy wedding. He'd drunk too much and starting pawing the bride. Since everyone else was drunk too, no one knew who'd knifed the German. The entire wedding party was rounded up, taken to the cemetery, and shot dead, bride and groom included. So I ask you, how could the German authorities punish their own looters if they publicly burned people alive and shot them down en masse, in a ravine, as they did at Babi Yar in Kiev? The Babi Yar episode is well known, but I heard about the burning of Jews in Odessa only once, and that was from Pasternakov.

" 'For a whole month afterward, the corpses smoldered,' Pasternakov told me. 'It was only later on that they built special ovens, which were the last word in technology and had a good updraft. With these ovens, they could round up people, lock them in, and make decent ash out of them. But in 1941 it was all still amateurish and disorganized.' They took prisoners and detainees out of the Black Camp, Pasternakov told me. I'd never heard of a Black Camp. Perhaps there was a White Camp too? Anyway, they took these prisoners out, issued each of them a hook, and with the hooks the prisoners had to pull the charred corpses apart, then dig a hole and bury all thirty thousand of them. Even after a month, not all the corpses had burned up; here and there, chunks of human coal still retained heat and continued to smolder. And that was how Pasternakov sustained first-degree burns, right through to the bone, from some smoldering Jew or Jewess."

The steel tracks were hammered beneath our feet. Again Chubinets fell silent. Judging from the lay of the land, the train was approaching the station at Paripsy and its wonderful well. The burning heat and stench that wafted from the hell in Pasternakov's, or, rather, Chubinets's, story had given me a tremendous thirst, particularly for some fresh well water. Not that I expected it to be as pure as Chubinets said. Really pure wells are found only much farther off the beaten path than we were. Most wells were sunk too close to animal pens or the sites of other human filth–producing activities. No, springs with pure water, out in the woods, bring pleasure only to occasional wayfarers or to wild animals. I knew of such streams of crystal-pure water that issued from a pipe, hidden wells sunk by the hand of unknown charitable men who cared about just such lone wayfarers. Wells of this sort are built to last: the gaps between the timber frame around the wellhead and the subsoil at its chilly foot are caulked with pure, properly kneaded clay; and the frames are made of oak or alder, long-lived trees, with firm rims free of the cracks that let earth seep through and muddy the water. Among varieties of birds, it is the lapwings, even though they're marsh dwellers, who most frequent such pure waters. When you approach a well, the lapwings circle, crying, "Drink! Drink! Drink!" And there is beauty all around, bees buzzing noisily amid bright flowers, especially along the slopes of ravines, and the grass growing. . . .

But even as I slipped into this reverie, Sasha Chubinets began telling me about the countryside he had driven through with Vanya Chubinets, his walleyed friend, when they rode out to the abandoned brickworks in the village of Krivosheintsy, where SS men more liberal than their comrades in Odessa threw raw rotten potatoes and raw spoiled beets to the local Jews, reducing them to the level of pigs allowed to feed on putrid vegetables before being sent to the abattoir.

"When we drove out to the brickworks the next time," I heard Chubinets say, "a Polizei met us and said, 'Why did you bring more? You mustn't bring any more.' I said, 'I was ordered to bring more, so I did.' 'All right,' he said, 'unload it. We'll give the Yids one last feed.' That's what he said, and I knew what he meant. Vanya and I started forking the potatoes and beets over the barbed wire, and the Jews hurled themselves forward, grabbing for it. They had evidently got used to their situation, like animals in captivity.

"As I tossed over the vegetables, I felt someone's eyes on me, raised my head, and froze. How was it possible for a young woman, standing in that shit-stinking air, in that womb turned inside out, to preserve such fine features, such wonderfully gray eyes? She was like the Tatar's wife, like the woman on the Simferopol train, the kind who in normal life would be unattainable for a crippled peasant boy like me. Even now, that inequality lay between us, though I was now higher than she in society—higher, because she couldn't have been any lower. At least our German masters still permitted me to live, to perform the filthiest kind of labor, but she, because she was a Jew, was denied even this. And she knew it, this beautiful young woman who stood motionless behind the barbed wire, making no effort to grab the remaining potatoes and beets, as the others were doing. She knew that the sooner hunger sapped her strength, the easier it would be for her to part with life.

"Crippled men are highly sensitive to feminine beauty; we understand it better than anyone, much better than a good-looking male with a well-proportioned body and young bull-like legs. That is what my play, *A Ruble and Two Bits*, was about. Any intelligent and beautiful woman who wishes to be truly appreciated should fall in love with a cripple, no matter how repugnant he may be to her on the physical level, because flesh exists only to deceive and be deceived."

Did you arrive at this idea all by yourself, Sasha? I wanted to interject. But didn't. The Narrator's tale was too tragic a backdrop for sarcasm.

We modern writers are so rootless, our literary upbringing has been so neglected, we're such black sheep of the larger literary family we should revere, spoiled as we've been by the present generation of arrogant literary godfathers, that we can't stop ourselves from interrupting the lives and destinies of the characters we invent, interrupting at the most inopportune moments to moralize or make an ironic aside. The concept of Author has become far too important in modern literature. A so-called Author feels comfortable only during the course of an interview, which has truly become the main literary genre in the second half of the twentieth century. For the length of the interview, he's the Lord of All, the master puppeteer, dispensing wisdom and poetic justice on all sides. But pull the Author out of the limelight, leave him to nothing but his own devices, and he finds himself beset by a strange kind of jealousy: envy of his own creations, the characters, who can push him aside and tell the world things he would prefer not to mention. Take me, for instance: I constantly catch myself correcting Alexander Chubinets, or even talking in his place. And Chubinets, I imagine, is no less guilty in regard to his own characters. Yet deprived of our characters, how could we writers speak? All we could do is give lectures at conferences, hold seminars, and make dry jokes . . . as one of my women friends once did, punning on the words *essay* and the Russian acronym for sleeping car: *ess-vay*. Of course the sleeping car she had in mind was not the kind in which Chubinets and I were traveling as I listened to his life story, the ordinary tale of a citizen of our Eurasian land from the end of the last century. No indeed; she was thinking of a proper sleeping car, designed and built by Mr. Pullman, with luxuriously furnished *chambres à deux* and built-in toilets. Such sleeping cars are meant either for writing essays or for rendezvous with women, and the likelihood of my encountering Chubinets in one of them is very slim.

But encountering the gray-eyed girl Chubinets described, assuming she survived somehow and left the Ukraine in 1941 for Leningrad, or, better still, for Omsk or Tomsk—now, that's a possibility. Because even if irony cannot be banished from modern literature, and no matter how inappropriate it may seem in the face of that wholesale slaughter, the savagery of our times does not have the dimensions of classical tragedy. The gigantic scale of bestiality in the present age is not wrought by angry gods or enraged titans; it is the work, instead, of ridiculous little mannequins who dreamed up their theories in bars and coffeehouses. As a result, the mediocrity of the executioners inadvertently detracts from the victims, and while it may in no way diminish their suffering or make their death any less horrible, it nevertheless gives their fate a touch of indecency. The gray-eyed girl whose eyes met those of Chubinets probably felt this indecency, apart from a purely feminine modesty in the presence of a man.

"She understood," Chubinets continued, "that I loved her at first glance. I a crippled peasant, and she an educated woman from the city, a teacher perhaps, a doctor, or something like that, perhaps even an actress, but the right to live had been taken away from her. That made us two of a kind, at least for the few moments we stood looking at each other. When I saw that, though she was starving, she was not chewing raw potatoes like the Jews around her, I suddenly decided to ask the German guard to let me give her the bread I had brought with me to eat after work. The German was alone, the Ukrainian Polizei having been sent off on some errand. There were all sorts among the Germans, and this one seemed kindly enough. Sometimes when guards were leading columns of prisoners, even Jews, the stronger Jews who were sent out to work, they would let them pick up cigarette butts. So I went up to him, tipped my cap, and said, 'Sir, let me give that woman my bread.'

"I showed him my bread and pointed at the prisoner I wanted to give it to. The German looked. He said nothing, but deliberately turned his back, so I could do what I wanted. I went up to the barbed wire and stretched out my hand with the bread. I didn't try to give her my salt pork. After all, I thought, she's Jewish and will feel insulted. She took the bread, and I felt her fingers in my own. They were cold, like the fingers on a statue in a park in winter.

" 'What's your name?' I asked.

" 'Lena,' she replied.

" 'Aaah,' I said. 'I'm Alexander Chubinets. Maybe there's a message I can pass on. . . .'

" 'Write to Leningrad,' she began, but then thought better of it. 'But how could you write to Leningrad?'

" 'I've heard that Leningrad no longer exists,' I said. 'It's all water and stones. It's become a swamp again.'

" 'Yes,' she said, 'for me Leningrad no longer exists.'

" 'You eat that bread. I'll come again tomorrow. Be at the fence.'

" 'I'll come if I'm still here.'

"And at this, tears began filling her eyes, and mine too. We stood facing each other, on opposite sides of the barbed wire, and wept as if we had known each other for a long time and had loved each other, but now had to part forever. I think this was the one and only time in my life when a woman loved me. And what a woman—the kind you dream about at night, but even better. And oh, how I loved her. I stood and imagined myself dancing with her somewhere while a phonograph played in the background, for even though I'm a cripple, I know how to dance. Not the two-step, of course, but the tango or a slow waltz. I learned with a chair as my partner. I used to pick up a chair and dance with it if the radio played the right music. With a woman like her, I would dance not to the sound of a windup phonograph, but to the music of a jazz band at the soft-drinks plant. 'Look!' people would say. 'Look at the cripple dancing with that beauty!' And I'd be wearing a jacket, a tie, and a velvet vest.

"I don't know how long our love lasted. No more than five minutes, probably. Suddenly I heard a Polizei shouting, 'Away from the wire!' I swung around and saw him running toward me, with an arm band and clutching a Russian rifle—the Polizei were armed with captured Russian rifles. I looked at him closely and recognized him. He was from the neighboring village of Popovka, and I had been in grade school with him. Baidachny—a horrible kid, a rat, who was always calling me 'Ruble and Two Bits' and teasing me and butting me with his head.

" 'Don't shout, Baidachny,' I said. 'The German let me.' And I pointed at the guard.

"The guard said nothing, just smirked at me and then at Lena. He'd probably seen what was going on between us. The Germans are a romantic nation. They love the theater. And it isn't true that they have no sense of humor. They simply don't have our sense of humor, just as a pedigreed dog and a scruffy stray find different things amusing.

" 'Don't you lie to me,' Baidachny shouted, unhappy at being recognized. 'You gave that Jewess good Ukrainian bread.'

"Then he tried to strike her with his whip, but the barbed wire was in the way, so he started calling her the sort of filthy, anti-Semitic names that your average Ukrainian knows so well. He even aimed his rifle at her, to frighten her. When I saw that, I leaped at him and grabbed him by the throat. I realized how crazy this was, that I was risking my life, but I couldn't control myself. It might even be better if he kills me! I remember thinking.

"There have been occasions both before and after when I didn't want to go on living, but at that moment the feeling was particularly strong. And kill me he would have. He raised his steel-reinforced rifle butt. Once over the head, and that would have been the end of me. But the German stopped him, called him off the way a dog is called off by his owner. Before obeying, Baidachny punched me in the side of the head so hard that my ears rang. Then off I went, back to the village, with my head clanging, together with Vanya Chubinets, who had seen everything. I looked back to see if Lena was still at the fence, but she had hidden in the crowd of other Jews.

"Along the way, Vanya asked me: 'Why are you sorry for the Jews? We had to work our asses off for them when they were living in the towns.'

" 'I'm not sorry for the Jews,' I replied. 'I'm sorry for people.'

" 'I'm not,' said Vanya. 'Except for the children behind the barbed wire. The Germans are no good. Let's break into a German truck. It's easy. They stay overnight in the village, and the drivers sleep in their cabs. We can get into the back by cutting through the canvas hood, and take some food.'

"He was crazy, but I was in a daze, listening with only half an ear because of the ringing in my head, which wouldn't go away. As we rode on, the light began to fade, the color of the sky deepened, and everything around grew dark; we couldn't see. In those days there were no lights in the villages, no electricity; people burned candles and oil lamps, which scarcely kept the dark out of the house. Moreover, the Germans had ordered a blackout, and windows had to be hung with thick curtains. So when there was no moon, it was as black as pitch. But the summer evening was warm and silent, as they usually are in the southwest. I passed the reins to Vanya and slid off the cart.

" 'What are you doing?' he asked.

" 'Nothing,' I replied. 'What are you doing yourself? You go on. I'm taking a walk. I need to walk.'

"When I was alone, I sat down on the ground, my mind a blank; there was nothing I could think of doing and nothing I could do. I glimpsed a soft thing flying around in the dark and realized it was a bat, a big bat. In our part of the world people hate them and try to kill them, particularly the children. But I love them, like I love frogs. It makes perfect sense to me that in the fairy tales beautiful women get turned not only into swans but into frogs as well. I remembered that when my great-grandmother used to console me for the nastiness of my brothers and sisters, who were now dead, and for my mother's indifference and my father's cruelty, she would talk about the animals that were mistreated by people. What she said made me want to become such an animal, even a dark bat like the one flying around so softly above my head. What an impossible dream, that I, with my bony legs and arms and my clumsy human body, clumsy even if it weren't a cripple's body, could ever fly. And this thought made me suddenly understand how dreadful it was to be born a human being.

"All of human malice comes from the fact that people are more unfortunate than a bat or even the lowest insect. Animals know how to take pleasure in the life they are given, right up to the moment they are squashed by someone's foot or killed with a stone. But we humans can approach the perfect peace of the insect, frog, or bat only in moments of great love, when everything else, all we care about, becomes a matter of indifference to us. Great love, however, does not come to everyone, and it stays so very briefly.

"Getting up from the ground, I walked back toward the brickworks, just as an animal would have done, with no plan or other idea in mind. I was like a bereft drake that circles back to the spot where his mate was shot out of the sky.

"Despite my game leg, I arrived quite quickly; Vanya and I had probably driven the cart no more than two kilometers before I got off. Short as was the time it took me, though, when I reached the brickworks I was no longer like a bird, but was staring fixedly, trying to determine what was going on from the winking torches and the orders being rapped out by German and Ukrainian voices. The Ukrainian was not in the local accent; it was more a barking, curt, Germanized Ukrainian. I realized the sound was western Ukrainian, and a numb despair settled on me. I knew the Germans used our local Polizei for minor jobs, as guards and escorts, although they were perfectly capable of beating up and killing people once they got going. But if real shooting was needed, firing squads, they brought in the western Ukrainians, who had joined the Germans from the region we are traveling toward now. Zdolbunov, the L'vov area, around Rovno, and the Stanislav area, all that semi-European, Polonized, Hungarianized, and Germanized part of the Ukraine.

"There they stood, in a cordon around the brickworks: the hook-beaked members of the SS Galicia Division, as identical as peas in a pod, inhuman, like blackened steel, with their Magyar mustaches, black combat jackets, dark-blue forage caps, and tridents on their sleeves. They stood a yard apart, with only one gap, which was at the main gate. I saw black covered trucks lurching out of the gate, one after the other, driving through, turning, and swinging onto the main road. And there were captured open Soviet trucks too, one-and-a-half-tonners, in which piles of people lay beneath the legs of the SS men sitting along the sides. All this movement was taking place in darkness broken only by the occasional flash of lamps and torches. Suddenly, from the heap of bodies on one of the trucks, someone stood up, took off his cap, and threw it down to me. I have no idea why he did it, perhaps because I was the only one among all those people standing around the gate who wasn't in uniform. The cap fell right at my feet, and I had time to see one of the SS strike the man back into a prone position before the truck made its turn and vanished. I picked up the cap, but a Galician ran up and grabbed it from me.

" 'Sir,' I said, not waiting for him to question me. If

I did not get in my story before he started talking, it would be the worst for me. 'Sir, my name is Chubinets, and I am from Chubintsy, just down the road.'

"The Galician unsheathed his army knife, ripped open the lining of the cap, and felt along the visor. He must have assumed a note was concealed there.

" 'Why did that Yid throw you his cap?' he demanded.

" 'I don't know,' I said.

" 'Ah,' he said in a slightly softer tone, probably taking me for a village idiot. 'Did you come for the clothes?'

" 'Yes . . . for the clothes,' I replied.

" 'You should go to the gully at Popov Yar, then,' he said. 'Soon there'll be lots of clothes and shoes. Now, take the cap and beat it.'

"So Popov Yar is the place where my gray-eyed beauty lies among the flock of crows shot down that night. Where I come from, we have plenty of good burial places. It's country broken by a multitude of ravines and gullies with many different varieties of soil— plenty of sandy hills where pines like to grow, spots that are nice and dry and suitable for digging graves. Farther west the area of loam and shifting sands begins, more dangerous for a traveler on foot but better watered and useful for sinking wells like the one at Paripsy."

Paripsy was, in fact, the town where we were currently stopped, and we had been there for some time without realizing it. It was only when Sasha Chubinets had walked away from the dead crows, wiping the tears from his cheeks with the Jew's cap, that I came back to full awareness. I again contemplated the night beyond my window and managed to erase the image of that other night, the night of the brickworks at Krivo-sheintsy. And so Chubinets and I were restored to our railway car at Paripsy station.

6

THE NIGHT WAS warm, but there was a chill in the air. Given the climatic peculiarities of the southwest, there is nothing contradictory about this statement. A biting wind can suddenly spring up in the midst of warm weather, and you can easily catch cold. So even though the mildness of the nights seems to encourage you to walk around in an undershirt, I wouldn't advise it. Before descending from the train for our walk, both Chubinets and I put on something warm: I, my suit jacket, and he, his sporty jacket. Warmed as we'd been by the work of storytelling, we had been sitting in our rolled-up shirtsleeves.

Paripsy was like the climate, a place of rules and exceptions. Deserted, dark, and quiet, but from time to time noisy figures appeared. Several women from our train passed, speaking too loudly for the time of night and rattling milk cans as they walked. Then two station employees walked by, also talking loudly, their flashlights gleaming. Falling into the general pattern, Chubinets and I jangled the bucket as we drew it from the well, with the chain rattling, the handle squeaking, and water splashing as we noisily drank, snorting like thirsty horses.

Our fellow passengers had the ability to sleep through anything and to fall asleep in any position; they rolled over on their sides if nobody else was sharing the seat, or they sat up straight, with their heads thrown back and their mouths wide open, or they curled up the way elderly women do, their bundles propped on a suitcase, preferring to doze under the lights and in the noise of a crowded compartment so they wouldn't miss their stop by oversleeping. That was why the sleeping car was empty and why Chubinets and I were left in peace to get on with our story. In addition, people avoid empty, dark cars, afraid of the thieves who earn their living by riding the trains.

Five or six minutes of the fifteen-minute stop scheduled for Paripsy in the timetable had elapsed, but we had been told the train would stay here longer than usual, because we were so far behind schedule that other trains had taken our place on the track ahead. After a while, the bustle and commotion began to die down, people became quiet, the noise diminished and then stopped altogether. After drinking the water, Chubinets and I relaxed too, walking back and forth to stretch our legs after being cooped up so long. The water had tasted good despite the proximity of the well to the station. Obviously this well was looked after. It had a timber roof and a rim faced with stone, sloping toward a catchment. The water could have been surface water, rather than that springing from a deep artesian source, but it was all the more natural and fresh if it was. It smelled of rain and stone—gravel or cobblestones of the kind used as filters.

I began to watch a man carrying a sack over his shoulder. From the careful way he moved along the platform, trying not to wake the sleeping passengers, it was obvious he was a thief. An honest man with nothing to hide speaks loudly in the night, bumps into things, blows his nose, and so on. My theory was proved: the man stopped in front of me and offered to sell me some automobile headlights. I told him I was not in need of headlights. He then invited me to accompany him to see some new wheels for a forklift. An electrician or plumber, evidently, who had been sneaking merchandise from his place of work. His pants were covered with brick dust. My companion, Sasha Chubinets, also took an instant dislike to him, and since Chubinets was not, like me, the contemplative Hamlet type, he made no bones about telling the man where to go. The plumber, who had no doubt taken me for a city slicker and an easy mark, was not pleased by this response. Seeing his hope of drinking money going down the drain, he turned on Chubinets and shouted, "You little snake!" and shoved his face with the palm of his hand. Chubinets lost his balance and staggered back, stuck his stick into the ground, but stumbled against the rim of the well, banging his shoulder. If the wellhead hadn't been so close, he would have fallen. Just like that, the situation had gone from general to utterly specific, from theoretical to perfectly concrete. Although, as far as incidents go, this one was rather ordinary, the kind you might witness on any street in the Land of All the Russias, especially at night. I grabbed the plumber's collar with one hand and his shoulder with the other. His shoulder muscles immediately bunched up, taut. But what does a plumber work with if not his muscles? It is not both hemispheres of the brain he exercises; that's for sure. And so, brain confronted brawn, and each flexed itself.

"Boor!" I shouted. "Apologize to this poor man." Then added, in a low voice, "Do it, and I'll give you three rubles."

"Seven," countered the plumber.

Why seven and not six, or ten, I don't know. Perhaps he needed seven rubles for his next meal or drink.

"Three now, and four after you apologize," I said.

The electrician/plumber, receiving his three rubles, let me twist his free arm. The other carried his sack. In this position I led him over to Chubinets to apologize.

"Don't twist my arm!" he muttered.

"Just a little longer," I gleefully replied, determined to get my seven rubles' worth.

Facing Chubinets, the man humbly began to apologize. "I didn't mean to . . . I'm sorry. . . ."

I expected Chubinets to react in Christian fashion, but instead he flared up, reached for his stick, and whacked the electrician/plumber, whom I was still holding. It was a good thing he hit his shoulder and not the sack, which probably had more than a dozen sets of headlights in it. That would have cost me plenty. As it was, I got off with a ten-ruble note. As soon as the man realized that he had been compensated for this extra trouble, he left without a fuss, without even a curse. A better Christian than Chubinets, though he didn't turn the other shoulder, because that was taken up by the sack of stolen headlights.

The total cost of our stopover in Paripsy was thirteen rubles. But in such situations, money is the least of one's concerns. I remember reading somewhere that Napoleon's first victory in Switzerland, at the battle on which his military fame rested, was actually won through a bribe and not as the history books say. A friend of Napoleon's, a Swiss banker, bribed the Austrian commander, and Napoleon took the fortress in question without having to fire a shot. When one is up against power and privilege, money is the cheapest way to even the odds. It should come as no surprise that the Jews, who have appreciated money since time immemorial, have a proverb to the effect that anything which can be obtained for money costs nothing. This explains why there is nothing more dangerous than an ideological murderer. His ideology makes him unbribable, and thus everything becomes priceless, from red-blooded patriotism to rotten potatoes—everything, that is, except human lives.

A society of ideologues and idealists, headed by an unbribable leader, deprives the people of the right to work and the right to steal, the former right being a necessary step in the acquisition of personal goods and the latter a necessary compensation for the fact that such goods are in short supply. Let us hope that our twentieth century has now put such societies behind it. One of them was smashed by external force, and another has gone rotten and collapsed from within, despite the pomp it displays to the outside world. But the story that Chubinets and I are telling is set in a time when both these societies were young dragons breathing fire in each other's faces.

Chubinets took some time to pick up the thread of his tale after we returned to our seats in the sleeping car and our train drifted off into the dark night, leaving behind the lonely platform lights at Paripsy.

"I'll never again permit anybody to beat me," he said after a long pause.

In his imagination, the thief had become a symbol. I recalled a proletarian poster that used to hang everywhere during the Age of Enthusiasm. It showed a worker hammering, with a kind of bearlike obstinacy, at a globe wrapped in chains. That's what the Union of Workers and Peasants is all about, a proletarian hammering at both hemispheres of our round globe. For him, the earth is a walnut, and if the heavens have been abolished along with the priests who purveyed them, then paradise must be sought inside the cracked shell, in the depths, in the womb of our Mother Earth.

It is in such explications of symbols that contemplative Hamlets reveal their talent. But that is all they are good for: philosophy for philosophy's sake, insight for the sake of insight, emotion for the sake of emotion. Hence their sense of futility, hence their to-be-or-not-to-be's. This is why we need the coarse tales of a Chubinets, with their low truths from a wounded gut and their striving to understand, without the benefit of a higher education, the murder of our culture.

"One evening," Chubinets finally went on, "Vanya came to me and said, 'I've found a truck.'

" 'What truck?' I asked. I had forgotten about his idea of robbing a German truck. But he hadn't forgotten; he'd simply been watching and waiting for an opportunity.

"The opportunity didn't present itself until early winter, after the summer of 1941, that summer of high hopes for the Ukrainian people. By late fall, most of the Jews of the Ukraine lay buried in ravines and sand quarries, a multitude of Ukrainian weddings had been celebrated in country villages, and Ukrainian organizations had been founded that were ready to assume power from the Germans. In Rovno, the center of Ukrainian nationalist activity, a Ukrainian newspaper called *Nova Sprava*, New Cause, ran a lead article by its editor, Seminyuk, that said the Germans had promised to make the Ukraine an independent state as soon as Kiev fell. Kiev was captured that September, but the promise was not kept. *Nova Sprava* then printed an article by Alfred Rosenberg, minister for the Occupied Eastern Territories. Entitled 'Hotheads,' the article said that Ukrainian independence was being postponed until the final victory. That was when Bendera's movement began, and the Germans started to arrest Ukrainian headmen and clerics and throw them into the camps previously reserved for the Jews. A call for volunteers to work in Germany was issued. Every farm and home was visited, and faced with sign-up sheets. If you said, 'I won't go,' they replied, 'Come to the meeting and say so out loud.' Those who did were forcibly, right on the spot, shipped off to Germany. But a few people didn't go to the meeting; instead, they ran away and hid. At the onset of winter, the Germans started a campaign to collect warm clothing and food for the German army. Supposedly voluntary, it soon turned into outright requisitioning.

"I'm giving you this general picture of the relations between Germans and Ukrainians up to the winter of 1941 so you'll understand why I agreed to go rob a truck with Vanya. It wasn't just an anti-German thing; we needed food, because after a summer of comparative abundance, starvation was upon us again.

"German vehicles were generally parked for the night in a group not too far from the road, but the one Vanya had chosen was completely alone. He whispered to me that two Germans were sleeping in the cab. Judging from its hood, this was a mail truck, carrying Christmas parcels for the soldiers—schnapps and sausage, maybe. Vanya was particularly interested in the schnapps. I was supposed to keep my eye on the cab and take the parcels Vanya would hand me from the back of the truck. We intended to throw them into a sack and, depending on circumstances, take them straight home or hide them in a nearby ravine.

"It was a windy night, and the roads were icy. I didn't think we'd get too far on ice like that if we had to make a run for it. I was terrified, but I really wanted some sausage and schnapps. I had nearly finished reworking my play, and planned to take it to town after the New Year and show it to old Saltykov in the town hall, and to Leonid Pavlovich, for whom I'd written the leading role, the desperately in love cripple. Since it was impossible to find a typist in the village, I'd been forced to write it out by hand, twice, once for Leonid Pavlovich and once for old Saltykov.

"So there I was, keeping one eye on the cab and the other on Vanya, who had climbed onto the back of the truck. He cut through the canvas with his penknife and stuck his head inside. All of a sudden, a hand appeared. It seems that a third German was there, keeping watch in the back of the truck. We had forgotten about the Germans' orderliness, which was not what we were used to on the collective farms. If two Germans slept, a third would stand watch. This third German proceeded to hit Vanya over the head with a heavy object. As Vanya slumped to the ground, rolling over and over like a log, I took off. Cripple though I was, I ran like hell across the sheet of ice. So many young men, teenagers and even children, were killed at that time for stealing, and I wasn't that young. If they caught me, I would have been executed as a saboteur.

"As I ran, I cursed myself for listening to Vanya. I couldn't go home, since I didn't want to put Aunt Steffie and her Russian in danger. I ran to the pond instead. It was extremely cold out there, especially with the wind blowing off the water. I walked along the bank, trembling from fear and the cold. Suddenly I heard someone weeping. It was Vanya, thank God. He hadn't been killed. He was lying on the ground, holding his head in his hands, having crawled there, because he couldn't walk. So much for schnapps and sausage.

"Fortunately, no search party was sent out after us. The German authorities had taken to entering the village only when they made a sweep; they no longer had anything to do with the local Polizei. Besides, why go to the trouble if we hadn't managed to steal anything? In the morning, they moved off, to deliver the parcels from the Fatherland to the soldiers. Meanwhile, Vanya's head swelled up like a caldron, but was as soft as dough. If you stuck your finger in the swelling, it left a dent. It took months for the swelling to go down. But by then I was no longer in the village. After New Year's I went back to the town, with two copies of my play."

7

"MY SECOND ARRIVAL in town was somewhat like my first, when I'd carried the note from Grigory Chubinets. I found that the enmity between Germans and Ukrainians was less noticeable there than it was in the country. The movie house was open, and both Germans and townspeople attended the showings. As for the town's theater, it was always full, particularly when operettas were playing, and Leonid Pavlovich was highly regarded, especially for his interpretation of the male lead in *The Merry Widow*. Of the male actors, he was the handsomest and the most experienced, and both a good singer and a talented dancer. Pan Panchenko, the mayor and a theater buff, recommended plays to the company and frequently attended performances. The German commissar, who had a slight knowledge of Russian, attended too.

"I no longer had a room in town, my basement having been requisitioned; so for the first few days I stayed with

Leonid Pavlovich and his blind sister. He read this latest version of my play with interest and thought it much improved. I couldn't just take it to the theater, however, because all plays had to be approved by Mayor Panchenko, who helped the theater in its work in any way he could. For example, he gave the company a play written by a local schoolteacher—supposedly the son of a kulak—which, Leonid Pavlovich said, was obviously autobiographical. The mayor ordered that the show be ready to open in three to four weeks, and threatened to send those who refused to act in it to a concentration camp. Some of the company were afraid to take part, because they believed the Soviets, our own people, would be back soon.

"When the Germans began to behave like beasts, the feeling became widespread that they wouldn't last much longer, that the Ukraine wasn't the place for them, even though their troops were still in the depths of Russia. Many Russians, even some of those who had once looked forward to the Germans' arrival, were now anxiously awaiting the Soviet army. Therefore they were reluctant to do the kind of things they might be punished for later.

"As soon as the mayor brought this schoolteacher's play to the theater, the chief producer, Gladky, proposed that the hero, Otava, son of the former kulak, be played by Leonid Pavlovich. But the actor prevailed upon Gladky, for friendship's sake, to let him off, and so Ivan Semyonovich Czech got the lead, with a pay raise to two thousand rubles, the same as Leonid Pavlovich. Czech had been asking for a raise for a long time and was happy with the deal. The part of Marika, the daughter of a landless laborer, was given to Lelya Romanova, the young actress. Mayor Panchenko came to one of the rehearsals, disapproved of Czech, and immediately called Leonid Pavlovich into the chief producer's office.

" 'I'm going to extend the rehearsal time for the show by another two weeks,' he said. 'You're assigned the role of Otava.'

"That was that, and Leonid Pavlovich got right down to work on his lines. I'll give you a synopsis of the play, since I was at all the rehearsals, observing the way Leonid Pavlovich prepared himself to perform in a play he didn't like, and wondering how he'd approach my play, which he did like.

"The play starts in 1929, during the period of collectivization, and shows the Communists evicting a family of kulaks. All their movable property is auctioned off, and the whole family—father, mother, son—is banished to a prison on the White Sea island of Solovetskiye. This actually happened during the first eviction of the kulaks. Collective farms did not yet exist, not on any significant scale, and the kulaks' fellow villagers, who themselves would later become victims of the campaign against the kulaks, dragged off the property of the first victims. In the play, the son, Otava, escapes en route to the north, hides for a while, and then gets work in a mine in the Donbass. However, back in his village there's a girl named Marika, with whom he's still in love, so he returns to his village. There he comes across a dreadful scene: the village's log houses are all boarded up, and the place is a ghost town. Starvation has carried off at least half of the inhabitants. The play is in two acts: the first is in 1929, as I said, and the second in 1933, after Marika's death during the famine. Otava goes to the cemetery, discovers her grave, and over it inveighs against those responsible. 'Why did you suffer?' he soliloquizes. 'I may have been the son of a rich peasant and you a laborer's daughter and poor, but who is to blame for the disaster that overtook you and most of my fellow villagers as well?'

"Leonid Pavlovich, despite his low opinion of the play, told me that this speech was a powerful indictment of the authorities, and, while I can't really recall how he played the role, when it came to the soliloquy, he always wept real tears, and more than a few members of the audience followed suit. Nevertheless, the play was coolly received. The Germans didn't understand it, although its schoolteacher author, who knew German, translated over a microphone. It seems that racists though they were, and capable as they were of trampling other nations and trying to wipe some of them off the face of the earth, the Nazis were baffled by the sight of a state destroying its own people."

I—Zabrodsky now, not Chubinets—consider this point an important one. Lenin may have been no Russian nationalist, but he was Russocentric. True, under his regime many Russians perished, but that was all part of the class war and a kind of sacrifice to ideals. Stalin's ethnic roots, however, were in the Caucasus. A Georgian, he used Russian nationalism for his own ends, but really hated everything Russian, everything Slavic, like any Caucasian tavern keeper. This is why Georgia never suffered anything remotely resembling the wholesale slaughter that went on in the Ukraine, during collectivization, for example. Stalin despised the people he ruled over. Yes, most of the prewar Soviet nation "loved" him because of the big stick he carried. The first few months of the war showed that much. That Stalinism would have collapsed had it not been for Hitler's crimes is an almost universally acknowledged fact. Collectivization and a reign of terror did not cripple the nation to the extent that the war did. Hitler's atrocities reduced the people to despair and turned them into Stalin's slaves—which they have remained to this day. That is why the rebirth of the Great Russian mind depends upon its release from Persian captivity. Upon evil driving out evil. The destruction of Stalinism can only be accomplished by Russian, Ukrainian, or Slavic nationalism— no matter how sad the consequences of that might be.

But enough, let us return to the tale of Chubinets, which I have again interrupted, so much so that he has fallen into a wistful silence and has opened the window and is looking out.

"Popelnya," he announced. "We're already halfway, and I've told you only a quarter of my life. I'll have to speed up if you're to hear everything before we reach Zdolbunov. A pity, but it's better to tell you the whole thing, even if I have to skip a little, than to leave off somewhere in the middle."

I agree. The measure of any life can be taken only at its end. Any part of a life, no matter how interesting, if treated separately, will die, like an amputated limb. So Chubinets and I did not get off the train to stretch our legs at Popelnya, but continued with the story we had begun—even though Popelnya is the largest of all the stops between Fastov and Kazatin. The station is a two-story affair with an illuminated sign saying RESTAURANT, a railway police office, and a stone out-house at the end of the platform. Not just villagers with milk pails get off here, for Popelnya is a junction, though a small one. People with suitcases climbed up into the sleeping car, bringing with them the damp predawn air. But when they became aware of the darkness and saw two silhouettes huddling in the gloom, they turned and left us in peace. Chubinets again took up the thread of his story.

"Unlike the Germans, the local audience understood the schoolteacher's play. But their reaction was luke-warm, except in two or three places, such as Otava's soliloquy in the cemetery, when sighs and the blowing of noses could be heard. For all the play's historical truth, it was artistically false, and ignored the unities of stage time and historical time. This was something I had learned from the Moscow Tatar and his beautiful wife. In a show, historical time is not what happens on the stage, but what the spectator brings with him into the auditorium. If, for example, a Soviet play had presented a scene of kulaks chopping up heroic members of the Cheka, audience sympathy would have been with the murderers, not the victims, because people had expe-rienced the miseries of collectivization. Now, as it hap-pened, the members of our audience were experiencing German occupation, so they secretly sympathized with the victims, despite the big red stars on the victims' caps and their long Jewish noses. Also, the mass slaughter of the Jews had somewhat silenced the average Ukrainian anti-Semite, and the usual ethnic jokes had become milder. Real anti-Semitism came back only with the restoration of Stalinism and the return of those Jews who had saved their skins by fleeing to Siberia and Central Asia. But Gladky committed an artistic error when he gave the slaughtered Chekists long noses, because many of the Germans had long noses and could easily have been mistaken for Jews. Maybe that's why, when the Germans began their general withdrawal from the Ukraine, isolated groups of retreating soldiers were slain by Ukrainians with all the gusto of a pogrom.

"Anyway, despite wonderful acting by Leonid Pavlovich and a touching performance by Lelya Romanova, the show was not a success. In those days, there were no dress rehearsals to decide whether or not a play should be performed; our German masters went straight to the premiere. The third performance was attended by the commissar and the local Gestapo chief, Herr Lamme, who happened to be redheaded and had a long nose, and looked a lot like my friend the Jewish tailor from Shepetovka. Neither liked the play, and they ordered that it be taken off. The commissar didn't speak to the chief producer himself, but passed his order down through the mayor. So Panchenko was forced to kill a show that he himself had promoted.

"At the same time, he became embroiled in difficulties with a group of Polish Ukrainians he had formed in an effort at Pan-Slavic solidarity. I happened upon this group through my girlfriend. She was one of the many young people who worked at the theater to avoid being sent to Germany, and also to earn a little money. They were used only for crowd scenes. Her name was Olga, and she was a Polish Ukrainian with flaxen hair and eyes of a mysterious gray-green or gray-blue color. Or maybe they changed color depending on the light, like the water in the cold lakes of Polesye, between Poland and the Ukraine."

Good description, Chubinets, I thought. I know the type well, naive yet cunning girls from the northern part of the Kiev and Zhitomir backcountry. Everything there is different from central and southern Ukraine. It is a low-lying area of unbroken, monotonous plains where the rivers flow slowly through marshes. The natives are sometimes called Poleshchuks, and they are unusual in both appearance and character. Chubinets's girlfriend's name, appropriately enough, was Olga Poleshchuk. Olga Poleshchuk of the cold gray eyes and flaxen hair. There's nothing mysterious in the reason she chose Chubinets: there were few men around. Few in the crowd scenes, few in the theater, and few in the town. The girls killed time either with Chubinets or at the Polish-Ukrainian music and drama club, where there were only two men, Pan Jaszczuk and Pan Saszinski. Rehearsals, Chubinets said, were held at Saszinski's apartment.

"They stood in a semicircle, all of them with sharp noses and all of them so much alike I couldn't tell which was Olga. Pan Jaszczuk played the accordion and Pan Saszinski was the conductor. The girls, showing their Polesyean temperament—outwardly slow but, underneath, combative—turned heads to the right, to the left, in time to the rhythm, music by Pan Jaszczuk, words by Pan Saszinski: 'Stalin and Hitler are cutting up Poland.'

"Mayor Panchenko had this idea of organizing visits by the group to German military hospitals to sing songs and entertain the wounded. But what self-respecting local Gestapo or NKVD chief would allow such a song to be sung, even in secret? So the group was disbanded, the mayor got a serious bawling out by the commissar, and Herr Lamme sent Pan Jaszczuk and Pan Saszinksi to a camp, admittedly of the labor and not the concentration variety, and he displayed leniency toward the girls. This was the moment, when the arts were under fire, that my play, *A Ruble and Two Bits*, was dropped on the mayor's desk. Leonid Pavlovich had recommended waiting. But how long can one wait? The Second World War had begun, one ideology had replaced another, and one set of bosses had scooted from their offices as fast as their legs could carry them, giving up their chairs to another set.

"Of course, I didn't take the play directly to the mayor—I had no access to him—but to old Saltykov. The former librarian gave me a polite welcome, but the joy he had displayed before the Germans arrived, when he had taken revenge on the works of Communist and proletarian authors and frolicked to the music of the balalaika, was gone. His wife, Maria Nikolaevna, who, as I've said, was the image of a well-born old lady from a Turgenev novel, had died of a heart attack six months previously. His dream of having the word *Yid* printed openly in the town newspaper had come true, but without any significant consequences for his personal happiness or the national welfare. Old Saltykov took my play, which the theater company's typist had typed out for me in return for two loaves of bread. I noticed when I gave it to him that his hands trembled like those of a sick man.

" 'I would like to bring you into our propaganda work,' he told me, 'as a peasant writer who has suffered and survived the horrors of Chekist collectivization. The Germans have freed us from Judeo-Bolshevism, but they sometimes fail to understand the peculiarities of our country, and their ignorance is exploited by underground Soviet propaganda.'

"The first time I went to see him, he was kind and open with me. When I went a second time, at the appointed hour, he raged at me and stamped his foot. 'If I had known what you wrote, I never would have let Mayor Panchenko see it. You took advantage of my kindness. The mayor shook your play in my face, and he had every right to do so. Just what are you trying to palm off on us? The lessons you got from the Jews in the Soviet theater were obviously not wasted. You churn out a lot of Jewish misery, and claim that your own petty physical problems are the problems of the whole world.'

"I said nothing. I was shattered—totally. Evidently softened by my humble silence, and from having vented his anger, old Saltykov exhorted me in cold tones.

" 'Burn this obscene trash yourself,' he said. 'Be a man and destroy it! Have the courage of a Gogol!'

"He meant what he was saying too. He took an alu-

minum tray, laid my play on it, and handed me a cigarette lighter. I think he had gone slightly mad from old
age, loneliness, and his other woes. This was the tray
he used for burning the underground Soviet propaganda
he was given to evaluate. With a heavy heart, I put the
lighter to the wad of cherished pages, not for a moment
forgetting that Leonid Pavlovich had the second copy.
Old Saltykov guessed as much, and made me promise
to burn it, along with my earlier drafts, and so ritually
cleanse myself by fire after the fashion of the ancient
Polyane tribe, our ancestors.

" 'What we need is literature that is actively opposed
to Judeo-Bolshevik propaganda,' he declared. 'Mayor
Panchenko is very bitter that the Germans banned the
play about the crimes of collectivization, but just between you and me, it was of no great literary merit to
begin with. But you—with your talent, you could have
written a far better play on the same subject.'

"We parted on friendly terms, but I went home as if
I'd just been at the funeral of someone I loved. When I
saw Leonid Pavlovich, he knew what had happened to
A Ruble and Two Bits without having to ask. As all three
of us—he, his blind sister, and me—were having tea
after his performance, he said, 'Sasha, I told you to wait,
told you that you'd destroy the play. But listen, I have
an idea. Three days from now, on Saturday, I'm acting
in *The Merry Widow*. I've been told that the Gebietskommissar will be at the performance. If I have the
chance, I'll talk to him about your play. The show is
always sold out, but I'll try to get you a pass for the
balcony.'

"*The Merry Widow* was a show that lured occupiers and occupied alike, as bright lights attract insects at night. And in the wartime world of those days, we were all insects of the night, both the kind that crawled and the kind that flew. The front rows were filled with officers' uniforms, interspersed with a few silk dresses; in the next rows were the uniforms of noncommissioned officers; then came soldiers, and, far back and in the balcony, the local inhabitants sat squashed together. All were there to enjoy a respite from the hell of war.

"There was a scraping of violins in the orchestra, a slow swishing of the red velvet curtains, and suddenly a trembling muslin world of butterflies and moths opened up before the audience. Handsome Leonid Pavlovich embraced the beautiful Romanova, and there followed the whole gamut of operetta vicissitudes. Tears welled in the eyes of SS officers. At comic moments, everyone laughed, regardless of racial affiliation, even the Gestapo chief, Herr Lamme himself. But, then, there were no Jews in the house.

"Beginning in 1934 and throughout the Reich, Jews had been barred from theaters and children's playgrounds. There was, nevertheless, one Jewess in our theater, and she appeared on stage too; this fact was unearthed not by the Gestapo but by its rival, the NKVD, when it emerged from the partisan underground and reclaimed the offices abandoned in 1941. She was Gladky's wife, an attractive young black-haired Ukrainian named Maria Gurchenko, who was marvelous singing Ukrainian folk songs. She was often in demand for tours with the theater's army-entertainment group, to sing for German soldiers, members of Vlasov's Russian anti-Soviet army units, or in military hospitals. She had only to begin singing the opening bars of 'Bitter Are the Tears That Flow' to cause tears to start streaming down the cheeks of any mass murderer in her audience.

"One day, Maria Gurchenko was denounced to the Gestapo as being, in reality, Manya Gurevich. She was saved only because the informer turned out to be Ivan Semyonovich Czech, who fled to join the partisans shortly after writing the denunciation. Gladky, with his patron, Mayor Panchenko, managed to convince everyone that the denunciation was nothing but a piece of disinformation circulated by the Cheka. And when the Cheka emerged from the underground, it believed its own disinformation. It's true that Gladky was under suspicion by the Gestapo, and, sensing this, he was always acting like a nervous lackey, fawning on the Gebietskommissar. You can imagine how he acted when the latter came to see him in his office after the show. I made sure I wasn't too far off, as Leonid Pavlovich had instructed me, and through the open door I saw Gladky all but lick the Gebietskommissar's boots as he drew up an armchair for him. The Gebietskommissar had a bottle of chocolate liqueur in his hand, and he called for Leonid Pavlovich. Administrators and secretaries scurried around, and soon Leonid Pavlovich appeared, handsome, imposing, still glowing from the heat of the last dance number.

" '*Ich gratuliere,*' the Gebietskommissar said to Leonid Pavlovich.

"Gladky poured liqueur into glasses like a waiter, tilting his head slightly to watch the angle of the dark brown liquid's flow. I was now standing among the junior theater staff.

" 'For the great actor,' the Gebietskommissar said in broken Russian, and then 'Prosit,' which in plain man's language means 'Down the hatch!'

"Leonid Pavlovich sipped with dignity, but Gladky tried to clink glasses with the Gebietskommissar, forgetting that glass-clinking is not a German custom and that he wasn't on the podium or at a banquet in the Town Soviet to celebrate the anniversary of the October Revolution. Then, apparently realizing his mistake, he got frightened and gulped down too much liqueur, choked, hurriedly moved to one side to avoid spitting liqueur on the Gebietskommissar's uniform, but tripped on the carpet and fell—who knows, perhaps at this point even intentionally, to amuse his master.

" 'Oops' said the Gebietskommissar, fortunately amused.

"Leonid Pavlovich cleverly seized this opportunity. He singled me out from the group reverentially crowded in a corner, introduced me, and asked me to say something about my play. Encouraged by his gesture, I began to talk, hardly knowing what I was saying, but in a great rush, mingling my own sufferings with those of my lame and infatuated hero. It got so, I had difficulty holding back my tears. Gladky, who acted as interpreter, had to signal me from time to time to stop so he could catch up in German. It was during these pauses that I particularly worried about bursting into sobs as I looked into the eyes of the Gebietskommissar, upon whom the fate of my play now depended entirely. What was worse, I kept seeing double, triple, or quadruple. His face expanded and multiplied over my entire field of vision. Then all the faces of the Gebietskommissar opened their mouths simultaneously and simultaneously flashed their rows of healthy teeth, and friendly laughter shook the crowded room.

" 'A cripple,' that multitude of mouths spluttered in unison, rocking with amusement, 'falls in love with a lovely fraülein. . . . *Jawohl!* . . . Oh, these Russian jokes . . . like Dostoyevsky . . . This *Unterhaltung* . . . cripple, on the stage, *müssen tanzen* . . . Oh, *jawohl!* A very *komisch* drama.'

"Such was the way my destiny took a sudden turn for the better. The Gebietskommissar issued orders for Chief Producer Gladky to begin rehearsals for a production of *A Ruble and Two Bits*. Leonid Pavlovich and I had just won a stunning victory."

8

———

"OUR VICTORY WAS total. I was immediately made a full-time member of the theater-company staff, with the grade of junior administrator and a salary of eight hundred rubles a month. I was given a ration card and a small room of my own. Leonid Pavlovich and his blind sister helped me to settle in, giving me household utensils and furniture. To tell you the truth, for me those were very happy days. Around me lay a town under occupation, in the misery and poverty of war, and with the sound of distant gunfire at night. But now that my play was being produced, I was in heaven. I tried to be at the theater as much as possible, and from there I'd either go straight home or I'd visit Leonid Pavlovich. Before that, I had sometimes gone to the movies with Olga Poleshchuk, but I stopped now. In fact, I stopped seeing her altogether, though after that disastrous business with the Polish-Ukrainian music and drama club,

I helped her get work in the theater, through the kindness of Leonid Pavlovich.

"For me the theater had become a dream world, a wall shutting out the filth of reality. Now, of course, I realize it was only a wall between one kind of filth and another. But I was young then, with a thirst for all that was new, and I felt servile gratitude to destiny. I attended the rehearsals, listening blissfully to the actors speaking the words I myself had written. I laughed at my jokes as they were told by Pasternakov in his Odessa drawl. I wept at my soliloquies as delivered by Leonid Pavlovich. I looked lovingly at Romanova, something I would never have allowed myself to do in real life, because she went out with Germans and was inaccessible to me even in my dreams. The theater artist made a poster showing Leonid Pavlovich doing a comic dance, kicking out a lame leg, while the beautiful Romanova and the cunning Pasternakov laughed at his antics. The poster was produced by the town printer. At last I saw my title, *A Ruble and Two Bits*, set out in gorgeous colored letters. The sight of this poster caused my self-confidence to soar, and for a while I became insufferably conceited.

"But actually, not everything was going smoothly— far from it. We made little headway, rehearsals were postponed, and then they were all canceled, supposedly because Leonid Pavlovich was ill. He really had come down with some ailment for two or three weeks, but rehearsals did not resume after his recovery. Frantic, I dashed off to see Gladky. He told me coldly that production had been stopped on the orders of Mayor Panchenko.

" 'I've always told Leonid Pavlovich, and now I'm telling you,' the director said, 'that Panchenko is a powerful man, and you'll make serious trouble for yourself if you rub him the wrong way. And Herr Gebietskommissar has no time for the theater any longer.'

"I soon understood what Gladky was hinting at. In the first flush of my theatrical triumph, I hadn't noticed that the Germans were getting grimmer and nastier.

"I was going home from the theater one day when I saw a truck filled with people in rumpled greatcoats and torn combat jackets. Soviet prisoners of war. When they saw me, several asked for a cigarette. I hadn't smoked in the past, but when rehearsals began, I took up the habit, and then I was never without cigarettes. I took out my pack and gave them the whole thing. Then they asked for money. I had six rubles on me, and was handing them to one of the prisoners when a German appeared with a dog. The dog leaped on me with such force that I fell to the ground. I could see the yellow fangs and soft pink tongue that would lick my blood once the dog closed its jaws on my throat.

"I'm afraid of dogs, particularly guard dogs. Do you remember my telling you about the Red Army dog that went for me? At least that one had been on a leash. Anyway, for some reason, despite the German's command, the dog wouldn't attack me. Maybe because German shepherds have wolf in their blood, and a well-fed wolf goes berserk only in a fight. It has no interest in a submissive throat unless it's hungry. So there I lay, staring straight up into the dog's eyes, which had suddenly turned from bloodshot to a kind of golden-brown color. The German struck the dog with his whip once, and me twice, then climbed into the truck, which drove away with the whimpering dog and the prisoners. My mouth was salty, filled with blood, because the whip had hit me across the teeth. Getting back to my feet with difficulty, I saw Romanova on the theater steps. She came up to me and gave me her perfumed lace handkerchief to apply to my split mouth.

"Although I knew she was living with a German officer, I mumbled, almost weeping from humiliation, grimacing in pain, and scarcely able to move my tongue, 'Our own people were bad enough. These are even worse.'

"As if she hadn't heard, she led me back to the theater to rinse out my mouth with iodine. It was after rehearsal time, and the theater was empty. I followed her into her dressing room, which was small, well furnished, and set up for two actors—the other being Maria Gurchenko, Gladky's wife. There I was, Sasha Chubinets, my mouth cut open, in a dressing room with Romanova. She sat me on her dainty divan, set a bowl in front of me, and quickly prepared a solution of iodine and water with her own lovely hands, pouring the water from a jug. I had never seen this fabled woman so close before, and she was tending *me*. I tell you, the bewitching effect of a truly beautiful woman is so much greater than the most romantic dreams.

"The iodine rinse eased the pain in my teeth and tongue, but my lips still felt as if they didn't belong to me. 'You need a compress,' Romanova said, and disappeared behind a fake bamboo screen. I heard her moving things around, the scrape of furniture, then an electrifying rustle of silk, and there she was before my eyes, in a dark blue silk floor-length dressing gown with lace at the neck and sleeves. Such a dressing gown was beyond my powers of imagination, because I belong to that breed of men who look at high-class women as if they were jewels in a shop window. Such men do not eye women's clothes; they look only at their faces and hair, and do not dare, even in their boldest dreams, to imagine the forbidden places beneath their garments.

"Romanova, seeing the effect she'd produced on me in her dressing gown, disappeared behind the screen again and reappeared with a bottle of genuine Moscow vodka, the very existence of which I had forgotten in the turmoil and tragedy of war. She doused a strip of gauze with the vodka and told me to press it to my lips. Almost immediately, the numbness went away, though the vodka burned my tongue and teeth. But this new pain was pleasurable, and everything that then happened was wrapped in a kind of effortless cloud. Removing the compress from my mouth, Romanova clinked her crystal glass against mine, and we drank, and followed that with some real Moscow sprats.

"After two, three, or maybe four glasses, she began to weep and complain about how terribly unhappy she was and how tired of the Germans, who, she said, didn't have any idea about how life should be lived. 'People think I'm a loose woman,' she went on, 'a German officer's whore. They don't know that I did what I did to save my mother, who was sentenced to death for being the wife of a Party activist. And now even Mother, for whom I sacrificed my honor, turns away from me.'

"We had a fifth glass, and Romanova, with weepy eyes that somewhat spoiled her beauty, confessed in a whisper, close to my ear, the disgust she felt when she was lying in bed with men who 'do not smell Russian, but stink of sickly sweet liqueur and chocolate. And their mouths don't move, and they taste of peppermint, and they'd sooner pinch you than get on with their business. My breasts and backside are covered with bruises.' With these words, she unhooked her foreign lace brassiere and showed me her breasts. They were remarkable breasts, with the pink nipples of a true blonde, and they really were covered with bruises.

" 'My husband, what a wonderful man he was,' she continued, moaning as she spoke. 'Vitya, with two blue tabs on his uniform and a lieutenant's stars. And what an athlete—why, he could pick me up as if I were a goose feather. And he would kiss me all over. Kiss me . . . all over . . . Oh, how I'd love to smell again the true smell of a Russian man. . . . Taste kisses that taste of vodka and onions and herring.'

"She kissed me, right on my lips, lips cut by a German whip, and pressed her mouth to mine, then drew back and said:

" 'Take off my panties.'

"The impact of this exercise in womanly wiles was like being whipped again around the head. But this time, instead of pain and terror, I experienced a kind of triumphant, almost savage power. It was like the force that had possessed me during the famine, when I felt an overwhelming desire to kill and eat a bird. The bird now was her delicate feminine panties, with their wings of lace, on her smooth thighs. I pounced on them, grabbed them, tore them off, while she delicately undid my coarse trousers with her slim and skillful fingers. After this, she sat on my lap like a little girl, like a daughter, on the lap of Papa Chubinets, the lame peasant. The rest is silence.

"Some men, as you know, in a tavern, when they've had enough to drink, like to dwell on certain kinds of details. But in a case like this, where everything was real, there is no need for details. In such a case, you don't ask yourself what time it is, or whether it has stopped raining outside. If you do, something's wrong. Yes, I have had occasion to engage in what medical books call the sex act, and was aware of every detail. But what happened to me with Romanova—and unfortunately it was for the first and last time in my life—cannot be described as any kind of act. An act has a beginning, a middle, and an end, but what I experienced then was a seamless whole, and while it was taking place I couldn't tell where it began or where it ended. And when it was over, there was nothing, really, to recall. What is there to recall when one first opens one's eyes at dawn? What detail describes the dawn?"

I have to agree with Chubinets. Not only do some men—and some women—shamelessly reveal every detail of their drunken experiences, but writers also write about them in their books, and this kind of writing has become fashionable nowadays, and profitable. I expect someone to write a play subtitled "A Drama in Three Sex Acts." And why stop at three? Thus we have an escalation, a competition, of lies. Lies, because such commercialized pap has about the same relationship to human passion as the squeaking of bedsprings. If even once in your life you experience what Sasha Chubinets experienced in Romanova's dressing room, you will never again pick up a pornographic book.

"And that," Chubinets went on, "was the premiere, the opening night of my play. Rewritten for the second time, but not by me . . .

"We parted in haste, because it was late and Romanova had to get ready for the show. 'Thank you for everything, Mrs. Romanova,' I said, and she answered, 'Just call me Lelya.' And added in a whisper, 'Our own people are coming. Let's wait for them together.'

"And so we began to wait for them together. Not literally together, of course, because I was never with her again, and we didn't even talk to each other. But occasionally our eyes would meet, and then it was clear that, yes, we were waiting together. And no one ever guessed that the only performance of *A Ruble and Two Bits* had taken place, with her as the heroine and me in the leading role of the lame lover.

"The next day, when I went to see Leonid Pavlovich, he said to me, over tea with saccharine, 'You know, Sasha, Romanova was drunk onstage last night, and when she began dancing, she fell. Fortunately, the audience thought it was part of the show. Gladky ran into the wings, and she cursed him like a sailor. She's beginning to regret being here. Indeed, we'll all regret it soon. When our people come back, what will we say to them?'

" 'I don't care. I just wish they would come,' I blurted without thinking.

"My lips still hurt, particularly at night, from the German whip, and several of my teeth were loose. Before we had parted, Romanova gave me a half-pint bottle of the Moscow vodka to use with compresses. But I didn't want to waste it and figured that the pain would go away by itself sooner or later. Besides, I had decided to keep the bottle as a memento of my wonderful premiere."

At this point, Chubinets was interrupted by the buffers as they clanked together in applause. But since iron is indifferent to human destinies, I thought the buffers were applauding not Chubinets but a railway matter, such as the appearance of the station at Brovki. I was wrong. There was no Brovki outside the window, only the formless countryside. Men with flashlights were walking alongside the cars, calling to one another.

"We won't get to Zdolbunov before noon," Chubinets said in a worried voice. "And by then there won't be any room in the hotel. I deliberately took the night train so I could get a room in the morning."

"I can help you with the hotel," I said. But Chubinets continued to look nervous, frightened, like a man with high blood pressure and probably a heart ailment as well. People with high blood pressure often become aggressive when alarmed, and, sure enough, when a short, thin conductor entered our car and shone his flashlight on us, Chubinets barked at him.

"What's all this nonsense? Why have we stopped?"

The runty conductor, obviously accustomed to bad-tempered passengers, quietly asked us for our tickets. As Chubinets showed his ticket, he continued to rage against the absurdities of railway regulations.

"What you're saying won't help," said the conductor, clearly relishing his ability to keep his temper. "What kind of railway is this, you ask? This is the people's railway. So instead of having a fit, sir, why don't you write to the newspapers?"

All Soviet officials, whether they be park attendants or train conductors, have a sixth sense about who can be pushed around and who can't. This conductor quickly pulled in his horns when I treated him to a dose of carefully phrased political rhetoric. Later I realized that it was not my words that impressed him, but my tan-leather English suitcase, which lay beside Chubinets's shabby briefcase and string bag. I decided not to press my advantage, however, because, after the things Chubinets had said, the conductor could report us. So when he turned out to be a newspaper vendor as well as a conductor, I bought a pile of papers and gave him three rubles. Again, as at Boguiki station, I had ransomed Chubinets.

"Why are you selling newspapers when there is no light in the car to read them by?" Chubinets demanded peevishly.

"You can read them in the morning," the conductor replied.

"In the morning I can buy a paper from a kiosk. These'll be a day old by then."

Chubinets had not yet cooled down from his account of the premiere of *A Ruble and Two Bits*. He clearly resented this intrusion of reality, and was impatient to continue his story.

"Why have we stopped here?" I asked the conductor in a conciliatory tone, hoping to put an end to the dispute.

"It's a restricted speed zone," he said, "under a Railway Board ordinance. The tracks need repairing, and there aren't enough ties to do it. I used to be the foreman of a crew that soaked ties in creosote, at the Kazatin chemical plant. And I was on an inspection team too. That's how I found out that somebody illegally sold fifty kilometers of ties earmarked for track repairs. On the black market, you know, you can get not only ties, but rails and plates, and couplings too. I wrote a report of the theft and sent it off, and this is the result: a trainload of people stuck in an open field. And now I'm only a conductor on the night train. Why? you ask. Because my nerves were shot, just like your friend there. When I'm better, I've been promised a job on the Kiev-Leningrad express. On that train, a person can sell sixty rubles' worth of newspapers on a single shift."

Remarkable, I thought, how open people have become, and cynical, in this post-Stalin period. Whereas the Chubinets type serves another purpose. People like him are instructive. We learn from them, the way scientists learn from a dog born with two heads or a calf that lives with only half a heart.

When the train at last got moving, Chubinets fell silent, and said not a word until we reached Brovki.

Perhaps he was annoyed with me for engaging the conductor in conversation.

"Here's Brovki now," he finally muttered "May it rot in hell."

"What do you have against Brovki, Sasha?"

Brovki's station was not very big. It had a fence running alongside it, was clean, and the moon shone brightly. The moon made me wish I were twenty-three again, and traveling with an eighteen-year-old girlfriend. But such wishes are futile: I will never get off a train in moonlit silence and hear the click, click, click of young Lelya Romanova's high heels as she runs to embrace me. Besides, it's not nice to make use of someone else's heroine; it's like climbing into bed with Madame Bovary. But at the moment, Chubinets and I were like a two-headed dog sharing the same blood, breath, thirst, and desires. Each a mirror image of the other, though on the surface one was grizzled and the other clean-shaven. But inside, we were a single dog, and so we would remain, until the mad scientist shut off the current and separated our minds.

"I had a bad experience here once," Chubinets said. "I was eating in the station restaurant, and some slob spit in my borscht. A jealous husband. It was good borscht too, rich, and with a piece of meat in it. The woman I was sharing a table with said, 'Don't pay any attention to him. Just pick out the spit with your spoon, and ask the waiter for a new spoon.' She said this very quietly, but I was seething. I picked up the bowl with trembling hands and took off after the husband. But there was an old man with a glass of fruit juice in his hand coming straight at me, and we ran into each other. I spilled the borscht all over him and scalded my own hand. On top of that, someone struck me in the back, a heavy blow. It was the old man's son—he had been behind me, and hit me with his suitcase.''

I burst out laughing. By the time I realized my mistake, Chubinets had got up and moved to the other end of the car, where he stood glowering in the dark. Now he was really offended. Fine, I told myself. I could have my brain and my heart to myself again. But it was too late: what had sprung into existence, with my cooperation, had now taken on a life of its own. I went over to Chubinets and apologized. In his life, few had ever apologized to him, and so he forgave me. Once again we began to share his life story, which, if the railway timetable was to be believed, had another four hours to go.

9

"IN OUR PART of the country, as you know, winters are short, there isn't much snow, and what we get doesn't stay long. I don't care for our winters. But spring is good, and it comes early. Summers are hot and muggy, but then in September it gets dry. In winter, the temperature falls to minus seven or eight Celsius, but there are cold spells that bring it down to twenty-eight or thirty-two below. You have to be careful in winter here. In 1943, I remember, the first cold spell hit us early—September 23. When I went to bed, it was drizzling, but later I got so cold that it woke me up. I tried to look outside, but the windows were covered with ice. Winter had arrived overnight.

"I leaped up and started rushing around, thinking that no matter what was happening in the world, with the war and politics, I still had to heat my room. I needed firewood, at least for kindling, because without it the turf I put in my little iron stove, which I had rigged up with help from Leonid Pavlovich, would smolder and go out. The room also had a beautiful stove of the Central European *kachelofen* type, reaching right up to the ceiling, with fine ornamental glazed tiles. But it was useless to me, because I had nothing to burn in it. Leonid Pavlovich advised me to dismantle it so I'd have more room, but I refused. How could I destroy the one beautiful thing in my home, even if it served no purpose? Maybe beauty is only beauty when it serves no purpose. The original owner, some wealthy doctor or an engineer from the sugar refinery, probably never even noticed this remarkable stove when he lived there, but simply warmed his back against it without thinking. I made a whole speech in defense of the *kachelofen* to Leonid Pavlovich one day. He threw up his hands in exasperation.

"Preoccupied with such domestic matters as these, I was unprepared for the disaster looming over my head. I went to see Gladky to get a signature on my request for a firewood allotment, to which, as a member of the theater company with the status of junior administrator, I was entitled. After reading through the application, Gladky said, 'It's all in order, but you won't have any use for it.'

" 'Why not?'

" 'We're reallocating your room to Pasternakov. He's an elderly man, in need, and he has that wound.'

" 'But what about me?' I was shocked but stood my ground. 'Where do *I* go?'

" 'To Germany, as a volunteer. You've been selected.'

"I thought he was joking. 'But I'm a cripple,' I said.

" 'So? There's a war on,' said Gladky, but he was not able to look me in the eye. 'And in wartime even cripples work.'

"At these words, I banged my fist on his table in despair. 'Then why don't you send your wife?' I shouted.

"He shot me a vicious look. 'Don't you dare hit my table. I don't know you anymore. You are no longer an employee of this theater. And your protector, Semyonov, can't help you, because this order comes directly from Mayor Panchenko. If you complain, it won't be Germany for you, but a concentration camp.'

"There was nothing I could do, nothing. Since Panchenko and Gladky had united against me, I'd be declared a saboteur if I didn't submit to this order. I thought perhaps I could explain to the Germans that I was a cripple and therefore of no use to them in the war effort. But when I arrived at the station square with my rucksack, there was nobody to explain to. I was merely part of a crowd immediately herded together by Germans and Polizei. In the group I saw Olga Poleshchuk—that is, she saw me and made her way over. Our relationship had ended quite a while before, particularly after my adventure with Romanova. But the present circumstances were unusual.

" 'You too, Sasha?' she said. 'We should stick together.'

"I thought, Why not? Olga had what it took: a fighting spirit. She went over and chatted with both Germans and Polizei, and learned that they were taking us to Kiev, the mustering point for the trip to Germany.

"Normally, it should have taken us twenty-four hours to reach Kiev, but it took us two weeks. We traveled in cattle cars and were fed measly rations of soup made from rotten beets and frozen potatoes. This reminded me of the vegetables I had taken to the Jews. We began to cough, catch cold, and suffer from diarrhea. To deal with the call of nature, whole crowds of us descended from the cattle cars and were led under escort into the fields. As the women squatted, the men turned away. The Germans were no longer treating us as human beings—not even as animals, because they kept their cart horses clean, and fed them properly.

"When we finally reached Kiev, we were housed in a building on L'vov Street that had once been a school. There was a barbed-wire fence around it. A transit camp, they called it. The men were put on the second floor and the women on the first. I wanted to speak to Olga, but I wasn't allowed downstairs. The guards were Russian women in black SS uniforms. I remember one in particular, a fat and vicious creature.

I tried to tell them I was a cripple—'*Ich bin krank,*' I said, not knowing the German word for cripple, but they could have seen that by looking at me. They didn't look, didn't listen. At a loss what to do, I sat in a corner and held my head in my hands, not like a person in despair but like someone trying to get his ideas moving, as if they were a cart bogged down in the mud. Because in such situations, all a man can rely on is his brain. I hit my head with my fists again and again, but no ideas came, and at last, exhausted, I fell asleep. Suddenly there was someone at my shoulder; I opened my eyes and saw Olga. She put a finger to her mouth. It was dark in the deskless classroom, and all my companions in misfortune were asleep. Olga pointed to the door. When I followed her on tiptoe into the corridor, she whispered, 'Give me the vodka.'

"She meant the vodka Lelya Romanova had given me. I had already opened it, because my lip cut by the German whip wasn't healing; it had become infected and oozed pus. Olga had helped me apply compresses in the cattle car to Kiev, so she knew about the vodka.

" 'But I need it for my lip,' I said.

" 'Just hand it over, and keep your voice down,' she whispered. 'I've fixed things. A German will let us get away in return for the vodka. Let me have it now, while he's on duty.'

"She took the bottle and vanished. I stood listening to my heart beat. Ten minutes later, she reappeared, wearing her sheepskin jacket, and hissed at me, 'Don't stand there like a jackass. Where's your coat?'

"I went back to my corner and picked up the sailor's jacket that served as my overcoat, and took my rucksack. Olga led me into another room, a classroom with desks piled on top of one another. They blocked the windows. We began carefully to take desks down and finally managed to clear a path to a very narrow window.

"I said to Olga, 'You'll never get through. Take off

your jacket, or at least the sweater underneath it. If you get stuck, that'll ruin everything.'

"She didn't want to take off her sweater. We argued. Finally she took it off and said, 'Go on now. Break the glass.'

" 'You break the glass. You're wearing the sheepskin,' I said. 'My jacket is too thin; I'll cut myself.'

" 'No, you do it, you're the man.'

" 'All right,' I said. 'But when it breaks, we wait. If nobody comes, we go through.'

"I pushed the glass with my shoulder. The window frame was strong, and held. I pushed harder, but it still held. Then I pushed with all my might, and there was a loud crack and the sound of falling glass. My heart thudded violently, and I struggled to keep from panting. But on the other side of the window all was silence. We jumped out and ran to the fence.

" 'Give me a boost up,' Olga instructed. 'When I'm at the top of the fence, I'll pull you up.'

"I didn't like this plan. 'It would be better if you helped me up first,' I said. 'I'm lame, I can't support your weight. My arms are much stronger than my legs, so I can pull you up quicker than you can pull me.'

" 'No, you help me up first. You're the man.'

"We began quarreling again and soon, forgetting where we were, were no longer whispering. Then we heard footsteps. Olga grabbed my shoulders, clambered up the fence, and pulled herself over. Before I knew it, she had dropped to the other side and was leaving without me. Meanwhile, the sound of footsteps was getting very close. In a panic, I ran without thinking, straight into a wooden guardhouse, like a wild animal stampeded into a pen. Luckily, nobody was there. On the table were a school pen and an inkwell. I sat at the table and thought, My heart is so loud, it will give me away. How long I sat there with my heart pounding I don't know, but it was already getting light outside when I glanced up and saw a little girl, about ten years old, looking at me from the street side of the guardhouse window.

" 'Mister,' she asked, 'do you want to run away?' In those days children understood everything.

" 'Yes, yes,' I said.

" 'In the fence, the sixth plank from the guardhouse has just one nail.' Seeing that in my terror I couldn't put two and two together, let alone count to six, the little girl went to the fence and lifted the plank, to show me. I crawled out.

" 'Are you wounded?' she asked, noticing my lameness.

" 'You've saved my life,' was all I could answer.

" 'Go as fast as you can,' she said. 'To the river. But don't go near the train tracks.'

"Ice had already formed on the Dnieper, but the river wasn't frozen solid. There was no way anybody could cross it, by boat or on foot. Staying close to the bank, I walked for a long time, even though I was completely worn out. Suddenly I caught a glimpse of someone's back, covered with chalk. It was Olga. 'You bitch,' I said under my breath. 'Bitch, snake-in-the-grass.' I

133

forced myself to go faster, and despite my leg managed to catch up. I didn't say a word, just silently kept pace beside her. The road was wet, and it was hard to walk. Olga had on boots that kept out the water, but my felt boots were soaked through. As Kiev disappeared behind us, she started making excuses.

" 'I thought the Germans had seen us,' she said.

" 'Bitch,' I growled, 'snake-in-the-grass.'

" 'This is no time to curse at each other,' she said. 'We have to go to the next village and find a place to stay.'

"We reached the village and found a cottage where the people took us in. They had us sleep on straw so we wouldn't bring in lice, and the woman of the house dried our boots on the stove. Toward morning we were waked up by the sound of shooting, and sat up like frightened puppies, clinging to each other. But the woman came and told us not to be afraid.

" 'Go to sleep, children. It's only Germans being killed behind the village.'

" 'Partisans?' Olga gasped.

"She had heard that the partisans in the forest would rape any woman they came across, five or six at a time. Her fear was partly justified, because such things had in fact happened, but it was also true that the Germans exaggerated the stories to keep people in a state of fear. Everywhere you went, you saw posters that showed a villager beating an armed partisan over the head with a cudgel in defense of his property and his wife.

" 'What partisans?' asked the woman. 'There are no partisans around here. It's only our men killing Ger-